Calypso George

Rea Rahaman

WORKBOOK PRESS LLC
187 E Warm Springs Rd,
Suite B285, Las Vegas, NV 89119, USA

Website: https://workbookpress.com/
Hotline: 1-888-818-4856
Email: admin@workbookpress.com

Ordering Information:
Quantity sales. Special discounts are available on quantity purchases by corporations, associations, and others. For details, contact the publisher at the address above.

ISBN-13:   978-1-955459-64-8 (Paperback Version)
              978-1-955459-63-1 (Digital Version)

REV. DATE: 25.05.2021

For my girlfriends
Deana Harris-South Wales, Great Britain
Shenaz Musfir-Cambridgeshire, England
Simone Fiedtkou-Leonard, West Virginia, USA

In memory of

Sophia Khan-Salah (1965-2007)
I know you are laughing.

Contents

1

The sun was beginning to sink below the horizon as the yacht pulled up about five hundred feet from the west coast shore off the Caribbean island of Barbados. The captain turned the engine off and dropped the anchor into the water. The seemingly endless horizon stretched over the countless ocean swells as the yacht had left the waters of the Atlantic Ocean and slowly drifted into the Caribbean Sea.

A man was standing with binoculars watching some birds making their way across the beach in search of food. They hopped through the sand and stopped to see what is in the sand. They peeked at a piece of something and realized that it was a live crab and let go, flew up to the sky, quaking and down the birds went again repeating the same behavior.

The salty tang of the ocean flew into orbit and landed into the man's loud laughter as he watched the magical kaleidoscope from the beach. The rumbling of the sea waves tumbled and cascaded towards the white sand, making a ripple effect, tugging at the drifting wood that lay afloat in the warm water. A few male birds hollered a mating call while the female birds sang a tune of ready anytime. In a few minutes, all was silent as the waves bound off the yacht and slowly disappeared into the ocean.

In the distant, way down below in the aqua water fishes swam annoyed at the disturbance the engine made upon the yacht arrival on a peaceful Sunday afternoon. A few locals looked and wondered who it is as they drove by in their cars from the beach to home or a dinner party. The captain joined the man and crew on deck to watch the last ray of the sunset disappeared, taking the yellow-orange glow with it. It was only six in the afternoon, however, the night is about to pay a visit on this island as it does every day. Silence prevailed as each male on board wondered what would happen next to the yacht and its crew. They sailed illegally in a foreign country, not knowing whether the country is hostile or peaceful.

The owner of the sixty-five-foot yacht let go of his breath as the last ray of the sun vanished into the night. This particular sunset is to be admired and it can never be capture on camera because it was one of those that "once in a lifetime sunset moment." He had seen many beautiful sunset sailing around the world in his forty-two years of life and yet he never shared one with a woman. He took the beauty of that moment all in and enjoyed every minute of it. He chuckled as twilight deepened into downy darkness and from within the deep blue sky a huge white full moon slowly rose over the island. It was too high to shine in any open windows or portholes, however, shine it did.

The owner of the yacht glanced out to the island and from what he can see it looked as if the whole island is lit not by the moon; by the power of electricity. He held his binoculars to his eyes, zoomed in to the house in front of him, and saw nothing. It was in darkness expected for one outside light; no one would ever have guessed a house stood there. He had seen it the minute the yacht drifted and anchored. He was drawn somehow to the bungalow sitting there with a pool in front of it. A strange sensation slid through his body and he shook himself free of it.

The silence was suddenly broken by noise in the distant waters. He turned his binoculars towards the noise and discovered it was an engine and recognized it to be the coast guard heading in his direction. He glanced around to see all crew members were visible and nodded his head to the captain. He hoped this is peaceful because he just cannot understand how in the devil's name his yacht is damaged when it was serviced before they set sail. Suspicion borrowed his brows together forming a frown on his forehead. This is the second time in four months!

The coast guards pulled up alongside the yacht with riffles. One of them yelled, "This is Barbados water ya sailin' in. Wha is ya business hay?"

"I'm the owner. My name is Liam Nwosu and this Captain Peter Lamburg and my six crewmen." The owner of Sincerity pointed to his male counterpart standing next to him aligning the side of the yacht, all hands on the rail. A standard procedure whenever they are on foreign land. "We have a problem with the engine. We are sorry to intrude, we've no choice. I would like permission to stay in your country and fix the engine, then we'll be on our way." Worry entered his tone, regardless he tried to keep it neutral and friendly.

The voice of the coast guard captain replied in a loud strong voice. 'I'm Captain Leroy Hinds and this ah Jerome Cummings and around ya is de army. We comin' aboard."

Liam raised his right eyebrow in a frown and lowered it to wonderment as he mouthed the word "Army?" to the salt air that engulfed the yacht. He wasn't aware of any other boats in the area much less the army. Damn it, he was in shock when he looked to his right and then left and saw nothing. He lift his eyes to the binoculars and lower them to level parallel to the horizon on the Atlantic side of the island and in the distant shore he saw the truck parked with a few men in uniform and the sea, he saw lights for the first time in another coast guard's boat similar to Captain Hinds'.

Liam had a feeling the army was around the yacht which he nodded to a crew and moved his head to the right indicating in their sign language to check the minute he can to see whether they are surrounded by the army. He couldn't move, as it would look suspicious to the Coast Guard and the army. Bloody hell, the army, this looks like a hostile island, then again, it may well be precaution, and who can blame them. He returned his attention to the two men who climbed aboard his yacht.

He watched as Captain Hinds, a short stout black man with a bit of grey in his hair extended his hand to him which he took pleasingly.

"Welcome aboard Sincerity. That's her name." "Tank ya man, but I need to see ya documents and passport for al' a wanna.........all of you." The stout man replied not in anyway friendly.

"Of course, this way, sir." Liam extended this hand showing him the way to the stateroom where all of his business was negotiated.

Captain Hinds nodded his head to Jerome Cummings a rather tall slim black man who stood with a rifle in his right hand, turned to match Liam's stride as they walked the short distance to the yacht's stateroom. An inquiring silence followed them; a silence that was too long to be broken. A sign of relief took hold of them both once Liam opened the door and pointed to a chair.

Captain Hinds sat where Liam indicated he should be seated next to a rich chocolate color chair with dark green and white stripes cushion and a tea table to match with the same color table cloth that also matched the cushion.

"Would you like some tea?"

"No thanks, this is not a social call." Captain Hinds replied seriously. "We would like to know why ya didn't call in your distres' befor' landin' in our waters."

"We tried several times and we received no replies. We guessed that our transmitter was broken. Our engineer picked up a cold in St. Lucia and he returned to New York. The Captain steered into your waters hoping someone will come to our rescue. Plus, it was easy this way as the tide was high and kept pushing us into these waters. Again, my apologies for any wrongdoing.... I didn't know what else to do." Liam finished looking helpless as his left shoulders took a rise to his cheeks. He was seated opposite Captain Hinds and he gave him eye contact as he finished.

"Wher' are you headin'?"

"We were headed to Africa."

"Africa?" Captain Hinds was surprised and showed it.

"Yes, we were sailing from St. Lucia after visiting some friends there. We were headed to Dakar in Senegal to refuel, then on to Accra, Ghana to visit some friends, and then to Burkina Faso, where I lived." Liam informed him.

Before Captain Hinds could ask any more questions the first crew arrived with his passport and the process begins of examining all documents on board. Captain Hinds contended that there were no threats to him and his country. He stood up and turned to Liam saying with a huge smile showing all of his crooked white teeth.

"Welcom' to Barbados. I suppos' ya know tha' I have to take all the passports with me and then return tomorrow with an immigration officer who will permit you to stay here. The army will keep watch for tonight. I suppos' you have enough food till tomorrow?"

"Yes, we do. Thank you. I understand and I will see you tomorrow after lunch." Relieve tucked into his voice as he looked at the island man.

"Oh, no sir, first ting tomorro', 8 o'clock." Captain Hinds informed him. "It's Monday, we will be hay."

Liam extended his hand to Captain Hinds saying, "Thank you so much. I appreciate all you are doing for us."

"I'll see ya tomorro' also with an engineer, too."

"Thank you, you are so kind."

"Not at all, glad to be of service. See you tomorrow." Captain Hinds made his exist, following a crewman, a tall slim built handsome man of mid-twenties, Peirce Fresh who lead him from the stateroom into his awaiting boat. He let his breath out as Jerome Cummings steered the Coast Guard boat into the darkest of the night. He was glad he was alive. Never can tell what the intention of people, could be drugs smugglers for all he knew. He came across too many of them drifting into the north Atlantic waters professing innocent, while their ship was sinking with marijuana or cocaine or both.

This Liam Nwosu from Africa looked honest and clean, however, most of the rich crooks usually do. Tomorrow will tell as the engineer and immigration will do their work and after that, it will be decided what course of action to be taken with them on the yacht. He made a mental note to run their names through Interpol and see what it would deliver. Tonight, he is going home and kissed his wife, better not, he will go and see the girlfriend and make passionate love to her. A smile of triumph tucked on Captain Hinds' lips and he was lost in thoughts.

Liam watched from the stateroom porthole as the coast guard boat disappearing into the darkness of the night. He let out a long-held breath and next took a few more to calm his anxiety. He walked to the bar and poured himself a scotch straight up as the yacht Captain walked in as he was swallowing it. He poured another and that followed the first. He looked at the captain, an eyebrow rose with a question on his face of "what is happening here, first the engineer," what's next, highlighted his face.

"Liam that was close." Captain Peter Lamburg, a stocky six-foot, salt and pepper hair with thick facial growth across his upper lips admitted venturing a comment and deliberately ignoring his boss's silent inquiry. He walked to the bar and poured himself a whiskey, plucking his mouth so that mustache did a little dance on his lips. He took a long gulped and swallowed. It hit the exact spot he wanted. He walked to the vacant chair where Captain Hinds was sitting not so long ago and put his weight into it.

Liam was standing with his back to Captain Peter Lamburg starting through the porthole into the pitch-black night. He turned to the Captain and said in a strong hard voice that gave an order to his question with no inquiry. "We don't have anything illegal on board, do we Peter?"

"No, Liam I checked the crew. I know sometimes they think they have the right to slip something on board but I personally scanned them and nothing. I asked them as well."

"Oh, all right. Let's have some dinner. I hope it's ready." He poured himself another drink and walked with the Captain to the dining room. Liam stopped in his tracks and looked at the house sitting all alone. He stepped back a few feet and looked again. Two lights were on, someone does live there. The six crewmen were seated as they joined them. The crewman, Orso Di Pa Squa, Liam had silently asked to check to see if the army was out there spoke before Liam asked the troubling question.

"Si, Signore d' army is outside." Orso Di Pa Squa gave his boss of ten years eye contact and quickly lowered his face to his food of spaghetti and meatballs with cheese. Liam acknowledged the answer with a nod and as he too was about to lower his face to the food taught otherwise as he remembered his drink, lifted his face and drain the liquor into his mouth. There was no doubt not to trust any of the crew as he had handpicked and knew them all for most of their lives. Orso Di Pa Squa hence "Square" came knocking on his door some seventeen years ago in Italy, filthy and crying. His parents had left him to fend for himself as they can no longer care for him. Orso was five years old and was asking to work for him. He took him to an orphanage to live in and send him to school; as soon as he was old enough he was riding the waves with him

Liam met the other four crewmen at different places during his vacation or when he was ramping through Africa and Europe in his mid-twenties. Peirce Fresh was nickname "Fletch" was homeless and wandering the street in Dijon a city in easer France where he was riding through to Switzerland. He was in his mid-twenties, he and five friends rode with their motorcycle across Africa with no problems. They hitched a hike all over Europe running out of money and instead of asking their parents to wire them a few hundred pounds, they found extra curriculum activities that lasted for years and had enough to start their own companies.

Onandi Natcho almost hit with his bike in Spain as he was walking in the middle of the road dehydrated and hallucinating from something that "Natch" as he called him never mentioned. He doubted he remembered the drama that put him in his path on that particular day he too was hallucinating from smoking marijuana. They took him to the hospital and the minute he was released he and his buddies who were riding as a group took him to a woman they heard wanted to adopt.

Jacasta Skandalis looks very Greek and short with wide-set shoulders. He was about nine working in the streets supporting his mother who was a drug addict. He never knew his father; Liam gave him his number to contact him in case of anything. Two years later while in a business meeting of some merger his private cellular phone rang. Cuzz as he was nicknamed by Liam due to his good-looking features which was a curse to other men, called to tell him that his mother died and he is homeless.

Xanthippos Xydis or "X" was a child soldier fighting a war he had no clue what it was about. He was stolen from his parents who later were killed by the rebels. Liam read about him in the papers and went looking for him. He paid the rebels handsomely for him; he was in no health shape to return home. Beaten with numerous broken bones, raped repeatedly, and undernourished he spend years in the hospital.

Jun Fujioka was not homeless, however, he came from a rich Japanese family. He didn't like the tradition he was born into and chose the life of a gypsy, a horror to his family. He was disinherited and Liam gave him a job;

he chose the yacht life.

In those days, Liam was a gypsy himself and a gambler. He studied, had sex, drank, and gambled. He had loads of money to upkeep all of the five crews and often visit them. Jun was one who introduced him to gambling when they were in Monte Carlo; Jun was there representing his family exporting business and he was for fun. They became friends and would visit the other four whenever they can as both of them saw to their education until they chose the yacht life.

Fletch was the deck manager, Square was the Chef, Natch was the housekeeper who has a multi-language degree as a translator while Cuz was the marine biologist and filled into different jobs as required. Liam and Cuz did many diving together and made a documentary for schools. X was the engineer as well as the pilot and each of them had medical skills to care for the other when there was an injury. Together they made great friends and work as a skilled team.

Captain Peter Lamburg was borrowed from a childhood friend and he never questioned childhood friends. As the Captain of Sincerity, Miles Quest applied for the Captain's job when Liam had Sincerity build eleven years ago, was on his yearlong honeymoon with the love of his life. The conversation was about the army outside and what the island held for them which they hoped to go exploring. Dinner was over in an hour and each of the men went their separate journey well aware of being watched, at least until the morning when they are cleared of all the illegal sailing into the undisclosed territory.

Liam walked to the bow of the ship and lit a cigar. He was tired, as it has been a long few days. He couldn't sleep. Lately, he has been irritated for no particular reason. Right now, he felt the last two weeks' restlessness and boredom with his life hanging too tightly around his body. He's on a suicide mission if he continued this way of life. He has been pondering what was missing since they left New York six weeks ago sailing the Caribbean towards home.

He had sailed this journey many times without difficulties. He knew something was not right as his instinct told him to be careful and pondered to be careful he did with on his instinct as he buffed his Cuban cigar. He couldn't even phantom a guess what could be wrong except that he had his feeling of carefulness haunting him for the last four years or even more, however, he caught it four years ago during a maneuver with a business deal. It baffled him then and it does now; parallel feelings with different experiences. It has been years since he had a long vacation, alone. Normally, he would've some friends and a woman to keep his company, no one special. He never had time to stand still long enough for a long term relationship. He had charted a girl of twenty-five for his consummated sexual experience at twenty. Oh yes, he knew the terrain of the female body more than he can remember. It had always been sex and business always in that order. He liked order as it gave him control and he stayed on top of life.

His relationship with women had more complex pathways than a beehive. He couldn't take the disappointment of their unfaithfulness, as he knew he wouldn't manage it well. He wasn't built for heartbreak. Besides, all the women he met are money hungry or a bitch or both. They used sex as a down payment to what they desired. Every man is potentially the highest bidder. Men seemed to cash in whenever the desire became overbearing or more often when they don't want to be alone for the night. He played the game, now he is tired of it.

Even being in the company of women made him felt lonely because it was always a sexual thing to pass time or quench the thirst in him and even that it didn't do sometimes. He never committed anyone as he could never see himself with any of them for more than a month or less. It was more of a problem taking any of those women to bed because they knew he was rich and demanded certain high prize rewards. This wasn't the issue as he always has one of many his assistants shopped for him. The conflict of interest gave him no pleasure in partaking in meaningless sex anymore. The release of his sexual tension had run its course and left him empty. He can feel the void in his emotions.

He bathed himself with rubbing alcohol to discourage any microorganisms from permanently moving in. It is time he found someone and settled down with maybe even have a few children. He is tired of going to bed alone. He wanted desperately to share himself with someone. Liam let out a long lonely breath as he watched the light in the house on the shore went off. His thoughts were into wonderment as to who lived there, returning to its former thinking of his life. Children sounded welcoming. He knew he would make a terrific father, and as for a husband, he wondered whether he could be a terrific one too. Who can he have children with? Someone who shared his value of not bringing them up with nannies and no love? He knew all too well of being with nannies and tutors with very little contact from his parents. He saw more of his grandparents than his parents. There was no other brother or sister to share anything with, only nannies and tutors. He grew up faster than most boys did his age. He challenged all of his frustration in getting "A's" and being the best at everything. He often felt abandoned, deprived of love, and very, very, lonely.

As he looked back to the place of his childhood and the last four years, he felt a restlessness, which he found disturbing. He felt the depression for a long time and started new projects only to add more wealth to what he already had which didn't make him happier. Liam realized he didn't enjoy his life as he once had. Something was unquestionably missing. He looked at the stars and wish upon them that he would find a partner to share his life with very soon. He drained his glass and headed into his cabin. As he prepared for bed, his thoughts returned to the Coast Guard and the island's finest keeping watch over them. Tomorrow is going to be a long drawn out day. He turned off the light and before his eyes were closed, he was asleep.

Liam was up, dressed and breakfast before Captain Richard Hinds, Immigration Officer Clive Cummings, and engineer Jeremiah Yearwood came aboard. He greeted and led them to the stateroom where coffee, croissants, and cream cheese awaited them. As soon as they were all served with coffee and the housekeeper Onandi Natcho left, Officer Clive Cummings, turned to Liam and asked him how he managed to drift into Barbados. Liam looked at Captain Hinds in wonderment as to why he did not inform the immigration officer of why he was here. Seeing the Captain's face buried in his cup of coffee he couldn't read his expression nor did he had any intention of communicating with him, he answered the question.

"I was on my way to Africa when we started to have engine trouble. Since the engineer was flown here to see a doctor, we had no way of figuring out what was wrong with the engine. About half an hour later, after the first signs of engine trouble, the ship shut down. We began to drift and we anchored here close to land. This is our first time here." He replied before taking a sip off of his coffee.

"I hope all ya and yo crew havz patient?" Captain Hinds spoke without looking at Liam instead his eyes were focused on the croissants. "It would be a long process." He continued more or less in a hungry lazy tone.

"Yes, we will, I understand." Liam voiced was pleasing, however, he wondered whether Captain Hinds would delay the immigration process just for the breakfast and wondered if he was hungry for the food or this is how the system worked here on the island.

"Good, Officer Cummings has your passport and he wishes to see each holder, just for precaution."

Liam was handed his passport. He opened it and saw the official stamp of entry for a week. Officer Cummings gave him an immigration card to fill out. Liam was about to fill in the information when Captain Hinds said, "Can you have someon' show de engineer Jeremiah Yearwood to the engine and Cummings will see the crew, in a different room. I wanna tak to ya."

"Of course," Liam replied as he reached for the intercom on the table. He requested the yacht's Captain Peter Lamburg to come and see him.

Immigration officer Cummings turned to Liam and stated, "Man I stamp it for a week and will do the same with the crew. I want that card back when I returned."

Liam nodded his head to the officer as Captain Lamburg entered the room. "Yes, Liam?'

"Captain please take the immigration officer to the crew in the game room and the engineer to the engine room."

Captain Lamburg nodded, "of course" to Liam, and turned to the two men and led them out of the stateroom. Liam took a sip of his coffee and watched Captain Hinds as he took a big bite of his croissants with cream cheese pouring out of the sides. He took a deep breath and exhaled slowly and very softly. His stomach was squirmy and that was because he had a bad feeling about this whole business with his yacht. He doesn't know what it is, nonetheless, he knew someone is doing something to him. Why now, before taking to the high sea? What did he do to deserve this? He traveled the world over and never a problem except running out of petrol, a few times due to the weather.

The first time Sincerity broke down was near Greece and he paid no attention or question why. The second time, this very feeling began to take shape as it happened in the Mediterranean Sea near Turkey. He told Peter to make sure it was serviced. Liam took the helicopter to a hotel and left him to take care of it. He flew to Las

Vegas and gambled his anger away. The third time it was in Australia and he left Peter to deal with it and flew to London where he stayed for a month living in a hotel. Now this, why? He made sure the yacht was serviced with a different company. He told this secretary to go to someone else and he listened to her while she made the call, what's wrong with this picture?

"I have a problem with ya story." Captain Hinds spoke and jolted Liam back to reality.

"What?" Liam asked in astonishment.

Captain Hinds wiped his mouth with his white linen napkin that had merged into the white of the table cloth and sipped some coffee. He looked at Liam and lay it straight to him. "Sir, somethin' fishy here. Fus your engineer left de huspitaal but did not fly to London as scheduled. He's still on de island, whereabouts unknown. I check you out with INTERPOL and they say that something fishy is going on with your yacht." Captain Hinds sipped his coffee and love the fact that he was in control of this delicate matter. He has quite a story to tell his girlfriend and the Prime Minister. He gave Liam his full attention. Looking at him straight in the eyes, he told him. "Are you aware that INTERPOL is investigating you for smuggling?"

Liam didn't realize that he was holding his breath. He let it out and returned the Captain's looking at him. "What?" In a shocked voice because he was shocked and happy that his instinct was correct to signal him of danger.

"Ya yacht, man, brok' down, 'his five times now."

"Four. I am aware of that and wondered why." Liam replied with full eye contact. His stomach was doing a summersault, nevertheless, he refused to subdue to any pressure. He didn't build his empire under any intimidation nor did he crumble under pressure.

"De suspec' ya of smuggling drugs and other artifacts like art and sculptures. I am not suppos' to tell ya and ya didn't hear it from me."

"Got it." Liam voice was strong and suspicious at the same time. "Smuggling? This is farfetched?"

"Ah kno' man, this is why a telling" ya? I had you checked out with a CIA and MI6 friends of mine and you wok har' and ya are fitly rich. Da is why it is fishy? Ya didn't hav' to do anythin' illegal, not for money, not for powa'."

"Thank you for telling me. What do I do from here? Where do I go?" Liam asked the Captain, still in shock. He was more concerned with enduring no breakdown of diplomatic relations with the Captain or any of the citizens of the island.

Captain Hinds realized he was in good standing with Liam and helped himself to another croissant with heavy cream cheese. Liam poured himself and the Captain some more coffee. Liam was thinking he doesn't need coffee, he needed a strong drink, scotch straight. He was in shock and wished his lawyers were here to deal with all this mess. He never had to go through any of this in his life before. This is why he has lawyers and paid them well to take care of his business. He knew what he should have done last night instead of thinking how unhappy he was, he should've called his lawyers.

As if reading his thoughts, Captain Hinds asked, "did ya call ya lawyers?"

"No, I will now."

"We are going on a manhunt for your engineer. Barbados is a small island so we'll find him, real fas'. We didn't know he was dangerous. Me thinks he had something to do with all this mess of ya shipwreck."

"I agree." Liam took another sip of his cold coffee and nodded his head.

"My suggestion' fo ya is to stay the week. Fix the yacht and leave. Get your lawyers to figa 'his mess out fo ya."

Liam took several deep breaths as he watched Captain Hinds put the last bit of croissant with heavy cream cheese into his mouth. He pulled a pen out of his pocket and filled the blank of the immigration card. He handed the card to the Captain and was told to give it to Officer Cummings.

"I guess you don't know a bad storm is coming here from Africa. It could be a dangerous hurricane."

Liam shook his head "no" and asked, "When is it coming here?" He vaguely wondered if this storm had threatened all week or was it a different one. The communication system was busted not long after they left St. Lucia.

"So far we know in two days but it can pic' up speed as if it was hell on wheels."

Liam laughed out loud and asked, "Hell on what?"

"Jus' an expressio' man. The hurricane can be a nasty one."

"Just what I needed."

"Listen man, here's my card. I guess you have food and water on board." As Liam replied "yes," Captain Hinds continued. "I'll come and check with you. We can have lunch and I will take you on shore but your crew remains on board. Do not mention anything I just tell you no one except your lawyers. Do not mention my name to them either. Da ya hea' man."

"I promise I wouldn't do that to you. I am very grateful for this. Thank you so very much. Please come and see me tomorrow and yes, we can do lunch." Liam said gratefully.

"Don't worr' man, we will try to help ya as long as ya don't involve me and my country, ya hear, man. Ah don't want no trouble from ya, man. Ah got ma hands full with this hurricane and other stuff to be bothda about smugglers. The seas will be full of all sorts of things." The Captain finished and pulled his full length onto his feet.

Liam did the same and extended his arm out to him. The Captain took it and shook it hard. He said to Liam, "Lead da way to de deck." Upon arriving on deck, they met up with the crew and immigration officer Cummings. Liam handed him the card and asked, "Is everything in order?"

"Yes, I give all of you a week to stay here. The army will keep an eye on you."

"The army?" Liam for the very first time since last night glanced out to the sea. His eyes scanned the surface of the Caribbean ocean and saw the brim of land with beach houses. He turned his body toward the left all around to where he was facing the officer and didn't see a thing.

"Oh, they left to change shift upon our arrival. Officer Cummings said in his slight British accent mixed with the island's twang. At the same time, engineer Jeremiah Yearwood and Captain Peter Lamburg joined the group.

"Well, something is absolutely wrong. Someone rigged the engine and wired it wrongfully to delay you at sea. I think because of the storm comin' the current pulled ya here." The engineer stopped talking realizing he is giving out too much information without an indebt inspection. He cupped his right hand and coughed. "Someone made a mess of things in there trying to fix things. I need to do a thorough inspection." He addressed the men looking at him. He turned to Captain Hinds. "I'll try and get it done before the storm." He turned to Liam. "Peter hay locked de door and change the combination so no one can git in. I took some photographs." He lifted his camera and showed Liam the shot he had taken. "I will e-mail you copies." There was no mistaking what his message was to the owner and crew of Sincerity. This isn't a regular inspection.

Captain Hinds turned to Liam and extended his hand. As Liam took hold of his hand; he looked up at him and was told in a professional voice. "We are goin' bac' for a briefing and I'll se' ya tomorro' mornin' at eleven for lunch. Someone will pick you up and bring you on de island." He turned and climbed down the ladder leading to the coast guard's boat. The immigration and engineer officers followed close behind. In the distance, another coast guard boat was speeding towards Sincerity.

Liam watched as the two boats stopped and exchanged

what he speculated was not only acknowledgment, also information, about him, his yacht, and crew. It's time to call his lawyers. Can he trust his lawyers? Who is doing this to him and why? These questions kept spinning around in his thoughts and he sensed a huge headache.

In the hours that followed, it was Liam's worse nightmare. His lawyers couldn't make it before the hurricane, as they were all busy with different projects and contracts. The earliest anyone can make it to the island would be after the hurricane into the next week. What good is that? Just as well, he made another call and asked for help about a delicate matter. His friend a retired Navy Seal mentioned he would call him at midnight. Liam was excited that he didn't mention his Navy Seal to his lawyers. He spoke with the crew and asked whether there is anything they need to tell him, any illegal activities about an incident as now would be the time to speak up. They all shook their heads as a "no" and asked why they couldn't go on shore.

"A hurricane is brewing," Liam answered him wearied and instead of relieved felt that he finally can quit wondering and truly do something about the mess someone is creating for him. Which hurricane was he talking about the one that hit him in his life and would worsen or the one that is about to hit the island? The yacht shook just then and the Liam trembled and next laughed out loud; he was afraid not only for himself, for his crew too. This was the first time something hit him that he doesn't know how to respond. This fishy business is getting to his nerves and he can't control any of it, maybe not now; he will soon.

"For real?" Crewman Peirce Fresh wanted to know.

"Yes. It might be a big one too so check the locks and food supply for a week. I want a list in an hour."

"Well, I guess we better make the most of it while we are here. You are free to do what you want except leave the ship." He concluded, turned, and walked back to his stateroom. He poured himself a scotch and tried to figure out who is using him and his company for smuggling. Who wished to ruin the architect of his financial empire? He always thought he had the world by his hands, now or the first time he is not sure. He was standing at his window looking out at sea when he saw a movement on shore, a female in a bikini. He removed his binoculars from his desk, adjusted the vision so that he can have a clear view.

Liam let out a breath with a whistle. He felt as if he was a "peeping Tom." He is a peeping Tom spying on the girl on the beach. What he saw he couldn't leave alone. The girl no older than twenty-eight in a yellow and white bikini was looking down on the beach picking up shells. No, not shells something on the beach, however, he couldn't make out the object. He scanned the binoculars up to her legs and felt his manhood reacted. He continued up to her front and was disappointed that he was unable to see anything and turned to her side. This didn't help him as she bent to retrieve something from the beach. A slight breeze whirled around her and the rain that treated the island seemed a distinct possibility.

Liam surveyed her stomach and was happy that it was flat. He smiled and he climbed the binoculars higher to her bosom and that was when he went all erected, making a sexual sound which came out through his lips into the salty air. All business of smuggling was forgotten. His eyes left the binoculars as he picked up his drink and took the reminding quarter glass; he swallowed and breathed heavily. Liam turned back to his window and once again lifted the binoculars back to his eyes.

"Where's she?" There was no one on the beach as he scanned the perimeters of the land of sand and rocks in front of him. There's no one; she disappeared much to his disappointment. Is he dreaming? He stayed for another half an hour looking for her hoping she would surface again. He can't take this any longer. He needed to cool off. He gave up, change, and went down for a swim in the Caribbean Sea.

2

Jamila Hassan made her way through the narrow white sandy path that led towards the beach from her bungalow. She took a deep breath of the salty ocean and exhaled, glancing at the yacht sitting on the turquoise water out some distance from shore; water lapping at it as if it was yelling "move out of my way. It has been there for two days and she never saw any signs of life. She heard the rumor about some rich millionaire anchoring outside her bay. It has been the first since she lived here that a yacht ever docked in front of her beach house.

The tide had come in and receded while she slept. The sand stretched to the water's edge gleamed in the sun's array as if it was pained in silver. Black-bellied clouds were threatening overhead and the sun kept playing peek a boo with them. A brisk warm breeze began to blow signaling the turbulent thunderstorms so common during summer due to sharing the month with hurricane season.

It's annoying because it blocked her view and aggravated her due to the pollution from the yacht. She hopes there wouldn't be any oil dumping or debris to poison the water. She had chosen this particular piece of land and built her cottage to fit the scenery. Her research told her that no boats, ships, and much fewer yachts sailed this close to shore or park at that particular spot. All floating objects go further south and not this north of the island.

She pulled the beach chair out from its hiding behind the bushes and laid her full five feet eight inches on it.

She hauled her novel out of her beach bag and opened the pages she left off yesterday. Halfway through the first half page of her mystery novel, she stopped a light reflecting off her sunshades, distracting her. She took her shades off and looked at it. Finding nothing, she resumed reading. Within moments, a shower of light reflected off the yacht and bounced off the screw at the corner of her sunshades again. Funny sensations she couldn't comprehend entered her domain. What was that? She felt the sensations ran through her body again. She ran her hand over her stomach and rested it on her heart.

She stared at the words trying to think. Someone on the yacht is spying on her. How bloody rude! She shifted her body and settled into focusing her attention on her reading. Slowly as if she has no control, her head tilted up slightly and she looked through her sunglasses at the yacht. She couldn't make out the person looking at her. What she could guess was that someone was looking in her direction through something.

She assumed it was binoculars. She pulled her body onto her feet and walked towards the bungalow. Upon arriving, she yelled for her friend, Damascus Paxton. A tall black man, with thin shoulders and narrow waist, shirtless, in shorts and with dreadlocks walked in front of her and spoke.

"Woman, wa' ya proble'." His black eyes wide with laughter, white teeth, and nose short and wide nose spoke in the Bajan twang.

She walked into the kitchen with Damascus on her heels. She pulled the refrigerator door open, took a bottle of water, opened it, and took a sip from it. She moved a few inches away and allowed the door to close automatically. Jameela turned to look at her friend, her voice hazy while her facial expression was annoying.

"Someone is spying on me from the yacht, Paxs."

"What?"

"Twice, I saw a light on me."

"Go back and continue doing what ya doin'"

"Okay, you are going to take care of it."

"Yep." The dreadlocks man replied nodding his head. "Don't I always.'

Jamila walked back to the beach with a bottle in hand settled it next to her in the chair, and resumed reading. She couldn't focus, therefore she pretended she was reading, turning pages. She was turning a page when a shadow fell upon her. Recognizing her friend, she turned and spoke. 'That was quick."

"Well, girlfriend it don't tak' much. It was a man tekin' in ya sweetness."

"What?" Her face turned red in shock.

"Yea man, it's a white man lookin' at ya." Damascus informed her.

"Guess he has nothing to do."

"No, the yacht is being fixed by Yearwood dis pas' two days. The owner was dining with the Prime Minister yesterday." Damascus informed her in his Bajan accent looking far out at the horizon beyond the yacht into the Caribbean Sea where the ocean stretched into the distance. He was looking for signs of the storm before the hurricane because he heard that it would be passing south of the island with a trajectory path heading into Florida towards the Gulf of Mexico.

'So, what's the story?" Damascus's gaze narrowed and he frowned as he left his thoughts and looked at Jamila. "Pete said that some rich guy yacht drifted da," looking into the direction of the topic of discussion. "The engineer got sick and was flown here but he never left the island to go to New York. The police went lookin' for him and found him in bed with a whore in Nelson Street." Pete was one of his many reliable cousins with accurate information. He works for the Ministry of Health as a nurse and knew everyone's business.

"Are you serious? Sound like something fishy, Paxs."

"Yep, Meya, me thinks so, too." He turned on his heels,

walking the path to the bungalow they shared.

Jamila returned to her book, however, she couldn't concentrate.

She gave up, put her novel down at the side of her chair, and leaned her head back. She closed her eyes and tried to picture the man who is looking at her. She became self-conscious and felt uneasy with the situation. She once again pulled her length onto her feet and walked into her beach house towards the sitting room where the telescope was and looked into it. She adjusted the lens to focus straight at the owner of the binoculars. She had a vision and quickly pulled away in awesome.

Damn, he's handsome, a unique handsomeness, she thought. If a painting could speak, this canvas spoke of the painter. She laughed as she spotted him angling the binoculars up and down the pathway leading to her home. He's looking for her. She moved the telescope from the bow to him and then down to the back of the yacht. There was no one about to expect him. She looked at him again, held her breath, and grasped. He is naked!

Or shirtless and his torso looks so ever strong with its slight tan and his nipples pinkish. His chest had little hair, just the way she likes it; she's hooked on him. A voice behind her spurred her into the present moment. "What ya doin'?" She jumped at the sound of Damascus's voice and threw herself into the sofa next to the telescope. Damascus laughter reached her and she raised her left hand and rested it on her bosom. Pink color stained her cheeks.

"Go find out all you can about him," moving her head to the left to look at her friend, "for me, will you?"

Damascus looked at her as black eyes met sparkling black eyes she added sweetly, "pretty please. I want to know who is spying on me, even if I wouldn't meet him."

Seeing no harm in the request, he nodded his dreadlocks head, "okay, be back fa dinna. Time for me to hav' some sauce, too. Teckin' the Jag." Damascus tossed over his shoulder at her as he left the room.

Jamila sat there lost and in wonderment. It isn't often she has someone looking at her while she's on the beach. She always had privacy. This is strange and a first. She didn't know how to respond or what to do; she was at a complete loss. She heard the Jaguar started as her best friend drove out from its parking. She had designed this bungalow exactly how she wanted it with both having their private quarters with adjacent kitchen. They shared the vehicle, a Jaguar silver sports car, and a Jaguar yellow jeep.

Jamila smiled as her memory journeyed to the day they met. Their mothers were best friends in school, one with Indian and the other with African heritage. Throughout the best friend's life, they shared everything even when they both became pregnant at about the same time. According to her mother, Amita who was married to her father, Kishore, a communication engineer from England, whose company was upgrading the communication systems in Barbados, fell in love and married in three months. They were both twenty-five.

A year later after she was born, her father accepted a promotion to work in London. Once a year they would return to Barbados for Christmas. Her father died from a massive heart attack when she was thirteen and her mother returned to the island, settling next door to her old friend, Mila who had fallen in love with her childhood sweetheart, Kai. They were married at the young age of nineteen. Amita and the Paxtons still lived next door to each other in St. George. Once a week, Damascus and she would drive there to have tea or dinner.

Her memory took her to the time she and Damascus would walk home from school, holding hands and singing nursery rhymes. They couldn't pronounce each other's names so "Meya" and Paxz were born and stayed. As the years passed, they became the best of friends. When she moved to London to further her education in business, Damascus stayed on the island to continue his studies, they would e-mail each other every day and talked once a week on the phone. She was there with him when he told his parents that he was gay. It was a rough and difficult time for her mother and his parents, however, within a year they learned to accept him.

They had planned to have enough money to live on before they were thirty. They worked two and three jobs during their college years and pooled their money together. Within two years they had enough money to purchase their first house on auction in London and sold it for profit. Damascus would visit during the summer and they would fix the house to look new and sell it. They worked hard during those summer months. They managed to purchase and sold twelve houses before they were bored and extremely tired.

Damascus learned the stock market and doubled their savings in a few months into the first hundred thousand dollars. They worked together and invested in a business that was in bankruptcy, building and selling it for a profit. Before they knew it, they were millionaires not a whole lot of millions; enough for both of them to live freely. They retired from work and sometimes travel together or alone, visiting the world. The backed packed from the jungle of Essequibo Coast of Guyana through the rain forest into the Amazon of Brazil. They invested now and again in one business or the other, mostly hotels and art where the revenue is higher.

She opened her eyes and jumped up as an idea hit her. She walked back to the beach and sat in her chair. She pretended that she was looking around the beach for something. She glimpsed a few feet to the right and witnessed the water of the ocean smoothing the rocks along the shoreline. She unexpectedly looked up and waved at the sailor on the yacht. A waved was returned to her, and then in sign language, she told him that he was such a jerk for spying on her and it was bloody rude. She was laughing and wondered whether he got the message. It never dawned on her that he may not understand the language then again not many people know sign language.

She had picked it up on a whim from one of her trips in Scotland where she met some deft children and wanted to speak to them. The week she was there they taught her to sign and when she returned to college, she took classes. It was a joy to see the children's faces when she returned one Fall day and signed with them. It was worth it. Jamila doesn't care whether he got the message or not, she folded her chair and hid it in the bushes. With her novel and water bottle in her hand, she gave a final wave and left the beach.

Two hours later, Jamila was seasoning four fish slices for dinner when Damascus walked saying, "smellin' good." Jamila looked up from seasoning the fished with a wide wicked smile. "How was the sauce?" A code they used for sex. Paxz visited his lover who worked for the government.

"As good as always, ya should try it sometim'."

"I know, I need to find a lover. It has been so long I am beginning to forget what it's like." She replied good-naturedly with a bit of sarcasm.

Damascus walked to her and kissed her on her left cheek. He told her as he massaged her shoulders. "You'll one day soon." He walked to the wine bottle that was sitting on the counter next to the salad bowl, took the glass she had standing out for him, and leaned on the cupboard. He filled his glass, took a sip with approval. "Good wine, Meya." He leaned over and filled hers as she popped the fish into the oven. She walked towards the salad and stopped as she remembered why he left in the first place. Reading her expression Damascus told her, "smuggling."

Jamila stopped fixing the salad and looked at him willing him to go on. Damascus continued, "someone is using him for smuggling and no one knows who. The police think that it's his engineer because the yacht's engine was rigged and in a bloody mess."

"Oh, dear." Jamila whispered. "I hope he gets out of this mess and not get pulled into it."

"I'm sure he's smart enough to do the math and figure it out," Damascus replied and walked outside to see the yacht. Jamila finished the salad and joined him. She automatically glanced at the yacht and saw no movement. She pulled a chair out and glanced at Damascus looking at her as he dropped his body into a chair opposite hers. "We need to get food and boarder up, cover the pool tomorrow. It will be a long three days. Oh, can you get some petrol for the generator and some liquor?"

"Yep, I figure it on my way home, people is shoppin' craz'."

"I will have the pool cover and tape the windows. I'll get the laundry done and have the house all ready by the time you get back for the shopping. I feel this hurricane is going to make a huge mess. I think we should leave and go to London for a week or two."

"I agree with you. I don't want to be caught in this madness. If the airport is open we fly otherwise we go to St. Lucia with the boat and fly from there."

"Good, agreed," said Damascus and with that, they both sipped

their wine looking at the yacht that blocked their view silently indulging in their thoughts.

The next morning at seven o'clock, Jamila was up and ready for work. The morning wind was kind, however, it was hot and sticky with silence everywhere "the calm before the storm;" the hurricane that came after the stillness of the storm. The last storm from Hurricane Mildred not only wiped out the generation of the black belly sheep; it took buildings and vehicles. Huge rocks tumbled down the steep mountain by Windy Hill in St. Joseph and it got steeper.

Hurricane Mildred rolled boulders from Chalk Mount Anticline down the climbers' path and shoving them towards the Cumberbatch's, Inniss's, and Greenidge's houses so close that only a very small child can walk between the boulders and the houses. It's a known fact that they ran out of their houses and hit in the bushes. The hurricane opened huge holes in the cliffs and moving rocks over by Ragged Point and shifting them towards Culpepper Island changing the geographic formation of Nice Beach and Bathsheba forever.

The scientific term for a hurricane is called tropical cyclone and because they are formed over the eastern Pacific Ocean and the Atlantic Ocean they are called "hurricanes." This hurricane name is Iffier due to the warm ocean that fueled the moist air which is a veritable hurricane refueling station. The surrounding areas of new air that has a higher air pressure pushed into the low-pressure areas and this new air now become warm and moist, so it rises. As this warm air continued to rise, the surrounding air swirled and takes set a course for joining together with other warm air that has already formed. As production is in full force, the warm, moist air rises and cools off forming clouds; water in the air. This manufactured more of the same and the system of clouds spin, wind, and grow which is being fed by the heat of the ocean as the water evaporated from the surface. It drives the storm into a hurricane determining whether it would have killer strength, part of a larger trend with wider wings and a huge eye.

It's a surfer's dream to surf before the storm. Surfing on wild waters made them felt the exhilaration of a high that they have finally caught the big wave. The danger zone of a swelling sea to toppled a surfer wish. Damascus and his cousins lived for these moments until he tasted the high sea of Hawaii and after a few tumbled with broken ribs he retired from surfing forever.

The merging sun was peeking in and out from behind the scattered clouds hovering with unbearable heat that it further mitigated by the sea breeze and the current of its spray. The dark black-bellied clouds rolled in blocking the sun, covering the warmth out for a few minutes then the sun came out and pushed it towards the other clouds with the same or darker characteristics. Outside storm clouds gathered on the horizon. The waves of the Atlantic Ocean and the Caribbean Sea pounded at the rocky inclined that ran from the beach. The green hills that rose huge on the other side stood tall and silent; not a bird swarm around them. Beyond the yacht, the deep blue waters flowed over the rim of the skyline. The scent of salt-washed the bow of the yacht and scrambled eggs sailed out the portholes into the air, landing only for a jiffy second on Jamila's nose. She sniffed the air a few times, however, the scent had gone and she automatically glanced at the yacht a dozen times.

Choppy waves crashed against the yacht rapidly moving onto the shore. The waves lined the water quelling internally with a storm of its own and lapped at the bottom of the yacht furiously moving it up and down. The salty water was a restless beast, prowling constantly who or whatever is in its path lashing against the yacht rocking it up and down, back and forward trying to sink it. For a few moments, Jamila wondered how they were all coping with the mess of what happened as well as the storm brewing. She saw the irony and wondered how the handsome man is managing.

Jamila was pulling the plywood out from the garage to stand next to the window when Damascus joined her and together they slipped and anchored them across the pool. Damascus gave her a quick wave as he hurried inside to shower and change for the shopping. He wanted to leave before the traffic became unbearable and the shops crowded with excessive people. Living on a small island they knew everyone and everyone knew them, therefore shopping or going out is a long process. Someone always wants a lift, or they stop to chat.

Jamila taped each window and closed the shutters in less than thirty minutes. She went inside to wash the laundry and tidy the house, pulled the candles, lanterns, and torches out, making sure they are in working order. She wanted it all done so she can relax. She stopped and glanced at the yacht; she saw movement and wondered who would be up this early. Maybe it's the handsome millionaire, up and worried about his life. She felt a tingling sensation in her stomach and couldn't comprehend any of it. She shrugged it off and continued with her work.

In three hours, everything was done, even lunch and dinner were all cooked. She was showered and changed into another pair of shorts and a t-shirt, her island dress. She flipped her laptop on and Google Liam Nwosu. The photographs that popped up caught her breath and she whistled a crocked no tune sound. "Fuck! He's a knockout of a hunk." She said out loud. She took in his forty-two years, straight long nose, hazel eyes, and black curly hair with a crew cut exposing regular ears. There's a light distinguish mark on his left cheek close to his wide thin lips. The smile from this photograph from Wikipedia shows very white teeth and a chin with a dimple in the middle.

There was not much information about him personally except where he was born, schooled, what he invented, and his businesses all over the world. He was almost a billionaire more than a millionaire. He owned flats in London, New York, Paris and homes in Burkina Faso, his hometown, Australia, Switzerland, Japan, Bahamas, and Argentina. A few photographs with him and four other males: Moroccan Clyde Zegaran, an Arab Adrian Bahar Al-Karachi, a Japanese Jun Fujioka, and an African Nyles Gilchrist riding motorcycles at various places in different countries.

Jamila's heart missed a beat when she saw the women around him in some of the photographs. The hard bone structure with firm muscles beneath the t-shirt kidnapped her senses and captured her imagination. She seizure the images and sealed them in her memory to keep forever. Her heart was rapidly beating sending her hormones out of sync; all she could do was sit there and faced the images that ramshackle her emotions and thoughts. She gasped and closed the laptop. "That's it, no more," she whispered loud and added a shrug.

"What's no more?" Damascus asked in a teasing glint. She jumped and turned around to look at him looking at her. Her hands went to her cheeks and she blushed.

"Well come on now, the bloody wind is picking up and we have lots of work to do." Paxz knew she had to Google the yachtsman. He can read her as if she's a book; she can do the same with him. This handsome yachtsman has his best friend intrigue and since very few males catch her attention; he's intriguing and that makes him curious. Females always have to know about things that are none of their business. There was no response from his best friend, Damascus headed to the kitchen to offload the groceries. They worked for the next hour; Jamila putting groceries into their rightful place, while Damascus filled the generator with petrol and started it. All the work was finished and they had lunch of salad, prawns with rice and peas.

It was soon after dinner that they heard the wind began to climb into hurricane force. The wind lashed brutally against the house, cracked in the trees, and almost lifted her off her feet as she was looking at the sky in the front garden. She ran to the front door and her friend passed her to park the car in the garage. She saw lightning forking downward over the hills and a slash of white whipped zig-zagging against the purplish-black background. Jamila walked out again leaning against the wall holding on to it, peaking at the yacht.

She felt the intensity of the wind as a clip of light showed the darkening sky as thunder roared. She saw the choppy water with massive swells hitting against the rocks from a barrier reef against the sea. The ocean stirred violently as this storm cracked thunder after thunder with bright razor-sharp lightning. A gust of wind picked up some leaves and tossed them about flying high above the roof of the bungalow; the rain dropped melted through the branches of the trees. Water and storm broke with blinding sheets of rain, blowing across the sea. Thunder boomed loudly echoing over them as Damascus drove the car into its garage and ran hurriedly into the front door. Jamila followed him both a bit wet from the pouring rain.

Jamila glanced through the kitchen window and couldn't see anything except the shutters. The storm driving rain against the window as Iffier picked up speed. This hurricane is getting worse and it's only four in the afternoon. It was playing havoc with everything in its path, the telephone and cellular phone soon went and the loss of electric power followed to the entire island. Candles were lit along with hurricane lanterns. Words weren't spoken as they both knew what to expect and what to do. They had experienced storms before, therefore this one wasn't a big deal for them.

The wind and rain are a mere introduction to a hurricane. An electrical storm before the hurricane is more dangerous than a hurricane on a corral and limestone island because it sweeps in and delivered a few random bolts of lightning, splitting trees in half and leaving things on fire. The storm picked a spot with high intensity of electricity and hovered over it for a few minutes, unleashing torrents of rain with crooked bolts of lightning, seconds apart or sometimes in multiples. It's known to pound away unkindly more common than the human species that battered the earth; as if the storm were an artillery barrage eliminated the enemy who has a different intention. Add some heavy gust of wind to this storm's mixture and the crooked bolts of lightning spread with the fire of rage to everyone and thing in sight.

Jamila settled into a chair opposite her friend and listened to the music of the wind outside. Before long exhaustion took over her and she was soon asleep. Damascus joined her an hour later. Several hours into the night, just after the eye left the island with rain pelting heavenly there was a loud sound on the patio's door that woke them. The voice was yelling, "help, someone please hell us." Jamila and Damascus came awake simultaneously with a jolt looking at each other through the candlelight. They both released a barrage of words best not mentioned, however, well known to mankind. It took another few seconds before the unleashing of words ran its course; they realized that someone outside their patio door was yelling for their help.

Damascus spoke first, 'Wait, I'll get the knife." He disappeared and within a minute, he returned and told her to move the plywood and open the sliding door. The plywood was placed inside against the glass sliding door in case it broke the glass, the debris of glass wouldn't come flying into the house Jamila did as she was told and wait a few seconds as her eyes adjust to the darkness before opening the sliding door to face the intruder. A very light summer breeze met her as she opened the door. The shock of seeing who was looking at her left her speechless and her mouth fell open. She blinked and stared at the "knockout of a hunk" at her doorstep. She swallowed hard and breathed in and out rapidly and even expelled a long breath.

After seeing through the lantern that Jamila held in her hands what was happening between the stranger and his best friend, Damascus intervened. He was the one who spoke to Liam because he was too taken aback by Jamila. This speechlessness and breathlessness is a rare commodity.

"What can we do for you?"

A gust of light flicked the lantern's light and he couldn't figure whether the hollow look on the stranger's face was a reflection of the aftermath of the hurricane or the anguish he's facing in his life or just the play of shadows from the candle's light.

"One of my crew is sick," Liam said and stepped back

to show them. Damascus stuck his knife behind him in his short straps and slide the door opened all the way, pushing Jamila to the side. He saw that the crewman was lying on an inflated waft wrapped in blankets on him. He looked at the stranger in the rain costume. Damascus spoke to Jamila without looking at her."Pull the table out so we can put him there." Jamila went and pulled the table that was between the two sofas out to the furthest corner. Damascus in the meantime was lifting the crewman from the waft forgetting that they were intruders.

Liam was looking at Jamila and couldn't take his eyes off her. He forgot about his crewman until the guy with dreadlocks inquired, "Ready." The crewman was put on the table in the middle of the living room. Liam deflated the waft, took his rain gear off, and looked at Damascus and then at Jamila with a question as to what next. Damascus walked over to him and took the deflated waft and raincoat with his left hand and extended his right hand to Liam.

"This is Jamila and I'm Damascus."

"Liam and this is Jun." Liam shakes Damascus's hand, however, he was afraid to touch Jamila. He wasn't sure what these two relationships were and didn't want to trespass; after all, he is in their house. He did take her hand which she was forced to acknowledge and reluctantly extended hers to receive his handshake. Liam quickly pulled away from his hand as his eyes met hers. Electrifying feelings drawled his hazel eyes staring into hers with confusing directness and he felt he lost his emotional balance. He hadn't heard her say a word. The silence was mutual and very sexual as the touch send sensations throughout both their bodies with neither being aware of the other.

Jamila quickly recovered as all eyes fell on the groaning man lying on the table. She disappeared and reappeared in a few seconds with the first aid kit. She kneed and took the thermostat out and put it into his mouth and under his tongue. "Jun, we are taking your temperature to see what's wrong," Jamila said softly to him. She looked up at Damascus and covey to him. "We'll put him in the back room." She turned and said to Liam. "You'll have the room next to his." The thermostat beeped and she pulled it out and looked at it. "106," she said. "He has an infection. How long has he been like this?" She asked Liam without looking at him; her back was turned; the reply addressed her question.

"A few hours mmm two."

"What did he have for dinner?"

"Mmmm chicken, he cooked it for himself. "No." Guessing what she was going to ask next Liam continued, "the chef cooked fish that he caught. Jun wanted chicken."

Jamila turned to Jun and asked him if he was sick before or after he ate the chicken. Jun opened his eyes slowly and looked at the girl hovering over him and barely whispered, "after."

"It's food poisoning. All the symptoms indicate it. Do you have a headache?" Jamila asked Jun the question to which he replied that he does. She pulled herself up onto her feet and looked at Liam and next Damascus. "He needs lots of water and I'll give him two painkillers. I'm going to get the rooms ready," she announced. Jamila took a candle and vanished into the back room to get it prepared for Jun. She headed straight for the bathroom and let out her breath. Oh, damn this, he left me speechless. Pull it together girl she ordered herself. She took three yoga deep breaths and was in control of herself again. In a few minutes, the bed all made she put the candle on the bedside and left the room.

"It's ready for Jun. I am in this one which is your Liam." A head turned in the direction of her finger. Liam nodded a "thank you" to her without giving her eye contact, nevertheless, she evaded his with a serious expression. She took another candle and disappeared into the room. She let her breath out and beginning taking sheets out to make the bed. She left the room without the candle and peeked into the back room. Jun was settled in bed and Damascus was giving him some water. Liam sensed her scent and became a wild mountain goat in heat responding to her with sexual sensation spelled in his dancing hazel eyes. He wasn't aware that sex was the message he was sending her nor was he aware that his smile spread his lips wide sending warmth to his eyes with a glint of light from the reflection of the candle.

Jamila felt a warm tingle dashing over her entire body and it felt as if it was déjà vu. Mysterious messages, however, sensuous they were carried on a current so resilient jumped in jagged voltage between them and made electricity look very weak. A warm smile automatically touched her eyes and returned to his hazel ones. Jamila headed into the kitchen taking deep yoga breaths as she walked. Damascus and Liam followed her and she jumped in the half-dark room when Damascus spoke.

"He is sleeping. I told Liam to check up on him and give him some more painkillers in a few hours. I'm going to turn the generator on so we can have the air-conditioning for the night. Keep the lamp lit." Damascus looked at Liam and Jamila staring at each other and left the room. This is going to be interesting. He can sense the sexual chemistry pouring through and out of them including the silent messages of what is to come. He decided he's going to have to keep an eye on them both. Liam, after all, is leaving and he isn't going to start something with Meya and then vanish to his world. Oh, no! She isn't going to get hurt by him over his dead body!

Damascus hit the switch and the generator kicked into life. He entered the kitchen to witness them looking at each other. Moments of quiet had grown and the sound of heavy breathing rent the stillness. Silence tickled heavily between them. They were in the same position he left them five minutes ago with a thick invisible electrifying connection that snapped tight between them. Besides the way the two meshed together, it's no telling what will happen, maybe it'll work out this time.

"Well, good night, you too," he said as he came into full view of them. He deliberately broke the trance they were stuck in and challenged Jamila to look at him. Liam also turned to Damascus and broke the sound barrier that evaded them.

"Thank you both very much. I truly appreciate it." Liam said in his deep sexy voice that made music in Jamila's ears.

"The hurricane has passed and what we are experiencing is the tail end of it. The wind has picked up more speed and the rain is beading down on the island. There's going to be heavy damage and flooding. Ya crew safe?" Damascus asked Liam in a slight island accent. The two of them were the same height; Jamila was about five inches short of them.

"Yes, the crew is safe under the protection of two police who is on board with them. They told me to come here for help. They said that you, Jamila would help Jun. They also said that if I do anything to either one of you that they would hunt me down as if I was a wild boar from Africa and cut my "previous" out and have it for breakfast." Liam looked at Damascus and refused to look at the most beautiful lady standing opposite him. She had to be smiling and he didn't trust himself.

"You're welcome. That sounds like my cousin," Damascus converse with a smile, turned to Jamila, and said to her. "You better get some sleep coz in the mornin' we're gonna have to do some cleaning up." His cousin, Clive, and his professional partner Elston are on the yacht. This is good because he'll go have a chat with him tomorrow.

"Goodnight." Damascus left them standing there as he walked to his room past the one Jun is sleeping in. He can feel their eyes on him and he smiled. He sensed that Liam is relieved that Meya and he are not a couple. Liam isn't the most handsome man he ever set eyes on, however, he knew from the look on Maya's face she thinks he is; she had dated better-looking men than Liam, nonetheless, the chemistry wasn't as intense as this one she shared with him. He knew his men and Liam is a sincere and trustworthy one; he's leaving soon.

Liam is overjoyed that Damascus and Jamila aren't together. He turned to her and smiled warmer and bigger one than his last one. "Thank you again and goodnight."

Before Jamila could reply, Liam was entering his room. She blew the candles out and left a lamp burning. It would save electricity for the air conditioner only. It's past one in the morning. How can she sleep now? She walked to her room next to the kitchen and headed to the bathroom to shower and cool her feeling too cold; it didn't work. Within minutes, she was in bed and started to laugh. She whispered under her breath. "Thank you, Clive." After a few minutes, she made a mental note to send him a gift basket for his thoughtfulness. Her thoughts relived the events of the intruders. She can't believe how attracted she is to Liam. It's a magical spell placed on them under the same roof together. She knew he's attracted to her as she is to him. Oh, dear, he is leaving, and she made a mental note not to get involved with him because there is nothing good coming out of the attraction.

Jamila can count the men she was involved with and that was not much. Most men she met wanted to have children as soon as they were married while she wanted to wait a few years. She refused to bring any child into this world she couldn't afford to support emotionally and financially. She somehow didn't trust anyone to be committed for life. The two men that she had a long-term relationship with, she realized that she didn't trust either of them to be there for her and their children. The first one cheated on her and didn't have the courage to tell her and the other one was a cheater too because he was forever comparing her to his ex-girlfriend or some other female. She found out after a year into the relationship. What's wrong with her self-value to choose cheaters? She wondered.

She trusted Liam for some unknown reason. Where is this coming from? Oh, no she thought as she remembered her girlfriend, Mavis saying something about twin flames. What was it, when you meet your twin flames it will trust at first sight, not love, trust? Soul mates have love, while twin flames have trust and true love. How ridiculous is this? Her sensations in her body settled, her thoughts hers, she understood what Mavis was jabbering about. This, whatever she has with Liam felt healthy and beautiful. What is so beautiful about it is that she knew he felt the same as she does; they have to figure whether they are going to keep it to themselves or tell others.

Keeping the feelings to themselves meant that nothing will ever come between them. Telling others meant that he would hang around and let the feelings developed between them and see where it will go. Oh, no she isn't going to do that, not her; she'll keep her cool and be a lady about it. He has a mouth and a warm smile he can say how he is feeling. If he wanted something from her, he's going to have to ask. Decision made Jamila turned over on her stomach, hugged her pillow, and was soon asleep with a smile on her lips.

Liam went to check on Jun who was fast asleep. He left and took the overnight bag sitting in the living room next to the table. He entered the room and to open the bag looking for his towel. He realized that it was opened and sorted through. Damascus had searched the bag or was it, Jamila? It had to be her because Damascus was always in view of them unless he did it before he went to his room or returned from the generator business. "Oh, well it's too late to think about it and who can blame either of them," Liam spoke to himself as he took his clothes off and slipped into bed. He jumped out of bed and pulled his briefs on. He usually goes au natural. Sleeping in the nude isn't going to work here. Can you imagine if she has to come in for something and see his erection? He had one the minute he saw her on the beach and it is still there!

What the hell is going on with him? He hasn't had sex in months, nonetheless, these sensations that overtook him is completely different from what he has ever experienced. Is she the one? His grandmother, Tahir, a college mate had told him he would know because it would be different from the rest of his lustful feelings. This is certainly not lust; it had to be true love. He was never compelled into speechlessness with anyone in his life. Yet, he stood there staring at Jamila as a lost mere "in heat."

"Jamila," Liam whispered to the howling wind. What an unusual name for an unusual lady. Is she a nurse, a doctor? How did she know what Jun was suffering from that quickly? She had to be a doctor. She is not the type to be a nurse. From what he figured, she likes challenges and his thought drifted to her shoulder-length black hair, dark tan, and soft skin. He knew her skin was soft, the softest he ever felt from the quick handshake. Her lips were broad with a squared chin and hollow cheeks. She had a short-rounded nose and sensuous almond shape black eyes. Liam had a wide smile on his face as the last image he had was of Jamila lying in his arms before he fell into a deep sleep. His appetite sparked at the sight of her. He was alive more than he had ever been in his life!

3

It was almost dawn by the time the storm lost its fury settling into a drizzle that lingered on for a few more hours before it passed and the sunrise. Finally, daylight with calm winds and waters; a stillness - the aftermath of the storm as the clouds is slowly blowing over and the blue sky showed its attributes. Sunlight chartered into the bed of Jamila about eight in the morning after the storm. She turned, stretched, and climbed out of bed. She looked for her silk robe and began walking toward her door. She was tying the cords of the robe together as she entered the kitchen and stopped dead in her tracks.

Jamila looked at Liam in shocking amazement, remembering her attire, and flounced back to where she came. She had caught in the gold of his eyes and her heart raced, warmth flooded her body, unintentionally she moistened heavily. Her heartbeats quickened, and her breath was caught somewhere between her throat and her lungs. Her knees buckled promising to give way to weakness.

Liam was leaning against the sink with a cup of steaming coffee in his hands. He was taking a sip from the mug when she bounced ten feet from him. He choked, not because of her entering and jolting him from his silence because she was naked under the robe. His heart was pounding over time and he had deliberately had no trespassing sign hanging on his heart. He welcomed anything from her. A smile entered his lips, a nudist, huh. This is getting better by the minute. This isn't fair, he had to wear clothes, why did she get to take hers off; as if remembering that it's her house and he is the guest, he felt the hot liquid of coffee burning his mouth. A sudden flash of warmth rushed on his face and his heart thumped over into his chest. The mixture of her reaction upon seeing him sank into the warmth of him.

"Oh, damn," he murmured.

"What?" Jamila asked as she entered the kitchen again. She looked at him closely only inches away. Her heart did a crazy little tap dance. She focused on retrieving a mug from the cupboard, poured the coffee from the percolator into her mug, and add a heaping spoon of sugar and cream more than usual. She was slightly trembling and had her back to him; he didn't see what she was doing. She looked at him as she anchored her body into a chair near the breakfast table. Liam had turned and looked at her. She had changed into a tank top and shorts with no bra. God damn it! Why the fuck this has to happen to him as he took in every inch of her. What the hell is he going to do? The fabric pulled against her nipples and beneath the thin cotton top, they stood at attention. He couldn't tell whether she was wearing panties, just as well. Worst yet she was unaware of it. Heavens what did he do to deserve this?

The scent of the energy that had drawn him to her in the first place was at this very moment wandering across the short distance that separated him from her. He was in total control of his body and thoughts before she came into his life again this morning, his ego told him. What a liar, his ego? Nothing is working in his favor. He can't even keep his manhood in control; the bloody thing has a mine of its own, behaving as if he's a teenager again.

She seemed composed, no different than cool water from a fountain, and in control! She gave her attention to the design of the mug and ignored him. She had bought it in India on a trip she had taken four years ago. The word Love in Hindi as well as the pronunciation in English "pyāra" was written on the mug. She unconsciously glanced at his mug only to discover "joy" was written in Mandarin. Liam was glad that she ignored him and took the minute to bring himself under composed. He never thought he would want to be ignored, however, he welcomed it until she glanced at his mug. He looked at her as he did the minute she entered because he had difficulty taking his eyes off from her.

"Good morning, Jamila, my mug read "Joy," what does yours read?" Liam sounded unsure as he managed that much out of his tight lips. He held her with his eyes. Sensing his discomfort, Jamila turned and looked at him with a bit of displeasure. His eyes glittered in the shadow light and her heart rates tripled. She was trying to be cool and in control and it isn't working. She looked at him, forced a smile on her lips, and said nothing then on second thoughts before she can move her lips to form what she wanted to say Liam's voice broke the barrier of silence that she had welcome.

"You can say something, you know, anything would be welcome than this silence," Liam said as a taint of an accent crept between his words. "It's time to bring some things out in the open." He decided on the spur of the moment to confront the intensity of energy between them, he wasn't afraid; actually, he felt courageous. Where is this coming from?

"Huh!" How dare him! Jamila noticing his accent and his nervousness and felt her more now than ever, "shut up the mug?" Her voice was a whisper and shaky. "Silence is good, especially when you invaded my privacy." Her black eyes were virtually spitting sparks at him. Those hazel eyes pierced hers with intensity.

"It was an emergency." Liam stated in defense of himself and on behalf of Jun." Although she accepted his reply, she couldn't control herself from being rude. It's self-defense of being protective of what? She couldn't figure it out and her voice broke even with words.

"Maybe you should leave and find a hotel."

"I will as soon as Jun is healthy to leave. I am sure you

can call a taxi. You no longer have to overstep……."

"I am overstepping my bounds. I earned the privilege when you came busting in here last night and dumped a bleeding man on me." Jamila yelled at him, a little higher than a whisper. It didn't anger in her voice only electrifying nervousness. "Besides, there's no taxi at this time."

Liam was staring at her and she did the same in return. She took a deep breath and looked at him with a smile that reached her eyes. "I am sorry," Jamila responded. "I don't like my space being invaded, particularly by strangers. Please forgive me, I am rude and…" She stopped and looked at him in his hazel eyes. She was lost for words then gathering her thoughts together they came up with a new idea. Finally, they are working constructively. "Maybe you would like to take a walk outside with me to assess the damage. How's Jun?" He nodded slowly his eyes trained on her body.

"He's over the worse and sleeping. Thank you for asking. I'll go with you. Where is Damascus?" Liam inquired.

"Oh, he left early this morning to visit our parents and see what he can do to help those who wanted it. He should be back any minute now."

"He left you all alone with us?"

Jamila laughed aloud. "He knows from the looks of you and Jun that I am not in any danger. Besides, where will you run, back to the yacht? There is no plane leaving this island and all boats are anchored safely. No one isn't going to get the okay to go anywhere from the Coast Guard until it is safe."

"Of course, how silly of me."

"Yes, how silly."

"I'm going to check on Jun before we, mmmm you and I leave."

As Liam walked off to Jun's room, Jamila turned and walked into her room for a quick shower and dressed in the same clothes with a bra and panties for the upcoming trip. Upon returning to the kitchen, she took the empty mugs and put them into the sink. She pulled two bananas laying looking depressed out from the fruit basket that was sitting next to the coffee maker.

She handed one of the bananas to Liam as he came out from the bedroom and they walked towards the front door. All doubt flew through the window when his hand touched hers and their eye met for a second. Liam opened the door and they stepped outside into the silent morning. He pulled the door shut behind him and followed her as she walked between some trees with broken branches. Beyond the house, she heard the sea crashing against the rocks to the rhythm of her heart. The rising sea of passion asked for a band-aid for a truly cracked heart because Liam would leave a huge black hole in her core.

They both were silent, not because they were nervous because they were occupied with the view, the damage the hurricane left behind, and eating the bananas. Broken branches and green leaves were whipped from their branches lay everywhere. Jamila noted some of her crotons and roses buses were broken and the tree she planted two years ago was broken in several places otherwise it was just another day of a wicked storm. It was wet and silent as no animals can be heard. A light wind, fresh with the tang of salt air from the sea blew across their faces. The brisk sea breeze wafted across the deck of the trees while another fresh breeze came in off the sea with a hit of freshness that promised to lower the heat for a bit however it did not serve to cool their heated body.

The beach floor was littered with the debris of twigs and dead branched that was broken off or fallen during the storm. A few times Jamila pointed to broken branches here and there, a lost bucket, a lost shoe from flying a long-lost journey sat in the open. Jamila stumped on some dead telephone wires. She stopped sullenly when she saw the live electric wires. She was looking around for a place to go when Liam ran into her backside. How he managed to do that she can't figure it out unless he had turned around looking at the path they came and didn't see her stop. Liam's hand came out and held her waist as she whispered softly "live wires" and automatically turned around to face him. He pulled her a few feet from the wires to safety. She looked up as her body fell against his as his hands held her waist firmly in place. He pulled her closer as his eyes sought hers.

Black eyes met hazel ones and the vortex of passion was unleashed into the essence of their being. She exhaled to her heart delight as a river of heat ran through her gathering moisture to deposit on her panties. Naked emotions are shown from his hazel eyes now trimmed with a bit of gold color around the pupils. His heart knocked solid and loud against his chest. He felt her body trembled responding to touch made'; his blood runs faster. Without further interruption, silence bestowed them. Liam focused on her lips and drove himself to distraction. He had an intense longing to devour them and then sample the voluptuous of her breasts. No, he wanted more as his hands tightened their hold on her waist. She turned to move in closer to him and whispered in his chin as her words pierced through his heart.

"Let me hide in your embrace."

"I hide in the peal of your beautiful eyes." He whispered as his finger lifted her chin to receive his kiss. Stroking her lips lightly with his, he softly let out a sound of joy against them, "you are in every breath I take, Jamila." He palmed the mount of her backside and pulled her into him. He used his leg to open hers wider and touched her pelvis with his thigh. She rubbed her pelvis into his thigh and music sailed deep from within her inner core. Liam lost his patience and pulled her bottom to his manhood and let her feel the hot strength of his arousal. She felt his excitement and moistened, pushing against him, automatically responding to him. Neither of them couldn't explain what they cannot understand themselves, so they let it be; let the energy forces that surrendered them propelled their bodies into a passionate kiss. The pleasing sounds that came from her charge him with a straight-up jolt of adrenaline flushing his body with heat, some sending both into an exotic rhythm of unheard music.

Jamila felt him against her pelvis just before he explores the exotic terrain of her lips. His tongue touched hers moving between setting them apart as he entered her softness and made a contract with her tongue. They collected each other taste as tongue touched tongue. A fire sparked, juices flowed, and all stand erect as they breathe life into each other's bodies. This vortex of passion in their kisses is hotter than Hurricane Iffier and helium fusion together! How long they were smooching is unknown; only a loud noise broke them apart. They listened as eyes crest the area around them and when they didn't hear anything, they began kissing again until the noise became louder. A scream pulled their bodies apart, more in confusion. It bordered on bizarre and they couldn't recognize the sound effects. It echoed as if a cat was crying as if the cat was under attack from another predator. They heard it again; a strange noise came from the ridge of the dunes of sand that was in a huge pile lying next to a fallen tree, in the opposite direction they were standing.

Two pairs of eyes searched between the trees and extended their ears listening to a low groaning. They followed the sound of someone in pain and saw nothing, only a narrow stretch of beach that bled into the tree line in the distance. Aqua blue line of the sea lay ahead. Liam took hold of Jamila's hand and pulled her towards where they came from a few minutes ago. Eyes scanned the right and left of them. Within a few feet from where the live electric wires rested peacefully, over some tall shrubs, they saw a man pulling a knife out of another who fell on the sand holding his stomach and heart.

Jamila grasped as a whispering sound escape her lips, however, before she could scream in shock of witnessing a crime and a man's death, because she knew where that knife when through that he would be dead in seconds, Liam pushed her onto the wet ground, covering her mouth with his hand simultaneously and lay some of his weight upon her back. Her head slammed into the hard wet surface of the sand and she felt the plates in her skull shifted two notches. They melted in the shadows of the tree trunk and held their breaths until the path was clear.

Through the wet hedges, they saw the man pulled the blade of the knife out of the other who was lying on the ground almost dead in a fetus position. The murder ran the blade of the knife across the fallen man's neck. They heard him breathe his last breath. Liam and Jamila were still as the island was before Hurricane Iffier. Not a whisper could be heard upon this aftermath of violence. All lies still as the man lifted some broken tree trunk and covered the body. He turned and looked around, seeing no one he headed for the beach and disappeared into the waters, knife loss at sea. Jamila whispered to Liam stammering "Is it safe now, you think?" He ignored the distance in her tone.

"I think so." he hesitated for a brief moment; sharpness entered his voice. He let out a long exhale and she followed. The images are frozen on their retinas as he rolled on his side. Liam leaned against the cold wet grass not believing the evidence presented to him. He would've done anything for Jamila not to witness what they just saw. He pushed his frame to his feet, pulling Jamila unto hers. They both stood still, looking around and noticing that no one would even suspect that a dead man lay there, some twenty feet away over the fallen palm tree.

"Should we see if he is alive?"

"No, he's dead. I know because I had a better view than you. He's dead and we have to get out of here." He shocked his head back and forth in a no format of no argument. "There's DNA and we don't want ours to be there. Let's get the fuck out of here. Where do you live?"

"De, beyond da' trees," she pointed and signed at the same time trembling the same as a leaf on its branch in the hurricane wind. A slight twang of her Bajan accent came tumbling out. Tropical storm number one with this sailor bites the dust ran from her thoughts into her spine and a wash of red color rushed to her cheeks. She stumped as her legs gave in to her feelings of shock. Liam picked her up in his arms and walked as quickly as he possibly can to her house. He put her to sit on the wet grass and joined her there. Neither of them spoke as they bought their breathing under control.

Unable to take anymore, Liam pushed his back upon the wet grass and pulled Jamila with him. She laid her head on his arm unable to move. He held her close to him. They both lay there shaking in the windstorm of their lovemaking. He saw the stormy emotions in her black eyes that blanked her face and he masked his expression. He wanted to be strong for her. Hazel eyes challenged black ones as he silently asked her whether she intended to report what she just witnessed; eyes locked into a spiral of silent communication.

Less than fifteen minutes or a little more, Liam pulled them into a sitting position. He lifted her and put her to rest between his legs as his hands held her around her waist. Jamila laid her head against his shoulders still composing her thoughts and trying to gain control. Strands of her hair gently blew into his mouth and bought him back to reality. He tasted her hair before he spoke looking down at her head. In an unguarded moment, a slow warm smile pushed his lips open. "I need a drink." Liam pushed her gently away and quickly from him. She looked at his face for signs of something, anything. She doesn't know what she was looking for, nonetheless what she found left her speechless. Suspicion laced his face and his body reacted violently. His head was turned to the side and he was keeled over to one side and exposed the bits of banana he ate not so long ago. She waited a few minutes, turned, giving him his privacy.

Jamila turned to him to make sure that he wasn't too sick and was incapable of taking care of himself. Satisfied with her assessment of the situation she stepped forward as another thought entered and then another. The whole image of a story came together in seconds. She had stopped trembling, turned, and looked into his eyes for assurance. There was an edge of frantic in her and she wanted to pepper him with questions. Her lips parted ready to ask if he knew any of the men, however, nothing left her lips. Having this failure to communicate only intensified her suffering. Reading her thoughts, Liam broke the silence.

"Why are you asking me?

"Is it your story?" Jamila managed finally, her voice shaking.

"Yes, I know the killer; he's Captain Peter Lamburg. I swear on my grandmother's grave I know nothing of this or what the hell's going on with my yacht and crew." Suspicion lingered in his eyes as he looked at her standing over him. He was sitting on the grass and she was standing a foot away from him and she sat automatically playing with a blade of grass, twisting and twirling it around. Poor grass it just went through a hurricane and lived now died in Jamila's soft hands.

"Yes, I think my Captain and engineer are partners in crime." Liam didn't voice his thoughts on which of his other crew was involved. He recognized that he is bigger than him and his lady love. He has to protect her, he wanted to protect her and knew he cannot because he doesn't know what the hell is breaking loose in his personal or professional company. He wondered who needs the protection most of him or her.

Jamila's eyes searched his for the truth and finding

them there, she nodded her head. She took several deep yoga breaths and finally said to him. "We have to tell Paxz. He would know what to do."

"Okay, after I have had a drink."

She smiled, stood, and extended a hand to Liam; he took it, helping her pulled his body up onto his feet. He allowed her to lean against him as he found comfort in it. His lips found hers and he drew her tongue into his mouth and marinated it with his own. "Thank you for trusting me. I promise that I will keep you out of this mess and protect you with my life. I want what is between us to grow and become something. This isn't the time for an intimate relationship for us. Jamila, I want an "us" Jamila!"

"I want that too." She whispered. She brushed her lips against his and as Liam was about to respond she pulled away teasingly, laugh, and walk away. He spanked her on her backside and took hold of her hand. They walked the few feet towards the door they left not long ago, laughing. They had answered to the gate of laugher and deep down they both knew that they love each other, however, it wasn't the time to mention it because there were more pressing things at hand to work through; a murder.

They were laughing and looking into each other's eyes when both hands landed on the door's knob to open it. Liam pulled her to him and kissed her. The kiss spelled everything to them, the longing, the fear of what's' to come, the pain of not knowing what would happen to him once they enter the door, and most of all they cannot make or demand promises that neither can fulfill. Jamila's heart thudded as sensations slammed into her with high intensity and warmth appeared she began to moisten. He allowed his fingers to dip beneath the fabric to caress one round nipple, while the other hand left the door's knob, sank into her shorts beneath the fabric of her cotton underwear, and cupped her backside. He jerked his hand back as the fire he felt send shivers through his spine.

Hell, he touched fire, the fire of passion. Liam didn't know for the first time in his life what to do with this fire burning in him and between them. Leaving each other would create a vacant place in their hearts. All they have is this moment and in the recognition, they treasured each other because neither of them knew how long they would be apart. They knew that deep inside where all the holes and hurt were that they would be there for each other as though they were blades of grass on a lawn. Liam put his hand on hers and let the door open.

Jun looked up scared. He looked at the two at the door and sick as he is, he knew the second they entered that they are lovers, his boss and his friend, his saver, a very sexy one. The bodies were unquestionably speaking the same language. They can smile across the room from each other and you can see the love they have between them. Jun felt it too. He was looking at them as an invader and they were looking at him in surprise. Silence bestowed upon them for a few seconds before Jun comment, "you can come in, I only launch here."

"Jun." Jamila and Liam said at the same time and stepped into the house. Liam following Jamila both giving their attention to Jun.

"Well, hello."

"How are mmmm I see you are, you feel...feelin' betta." Jamila stammered.

"Yes, thank you. I hate to impose on you, can I please have some food, no chicken, please. What is your name?"

"Jamila. Of course, a fish sandwich will do?" Realizing at the same time that she is hungry and so did Liam.

"Anything, thank you, except chicken," Jun repeated without any accent.

"In five minutes, it'll be ready," Jamila informed him.

Jun tiredly nodded his head, lead against the back of the sofa, and closed his eyes. He told himself that he will never eat chicken again.

"Good Jun, rest. I'll help Jamila with the food." Liam

is happy that his friend Jun is over the worse of the food poisoning followed Jamila into the kitchen. She turned and glanced at him with a smile that touched her heart.

Liam brushed her lips with his and took the few steps to the sink putting as much distance between them as the kitchen permit; both of them forgetting that their clothes are wet from the sand and grass. Jamila was there before he does and washed her hands. She moved quickly that his hands fell into space as he tried to get hold of her. She laughed and he grinned. He finished his journey to the sink. He stared out the window looking at the ocean and sky beyond the window. He spotted his yacht. The plywood had been removed.

Jamila watched him for a few more seconds then her stomach yelled for food. She pulled three pieces of fish out of the refrigerator, lettuces, and bread. She lifted three plates out of the cupboard, took six slices out of the bag of bread, and put them onto the plate. In less than five minutes, she finished the sandwiches and took Jun this with a glass of water.

"It's a fish sandwich." She informed him with a smile.

"Thank you."

She returned to the kitchen and seeing Liam's back to hers, she walked over and put her arms around his waist. She was fully aware Jun couldn't see them as a wall separating the kitchen and living room. Liam responded by moving his hands over hers. He pulled her closer to the middle of his chest. She heard his stomach yelled out to be fed. She laughed, pulled away, walked the short distance to the breakfast table, and handed him the plate with a sandwich and a glass of rum. He took the plate and laid it to rest on the top of the cupboard. He drank the rum in one breath and soon the empty glass joined the plate. He turned to wash his hands and saw a crab sitting on a small plate. He bent his upper body to take a closer look. Is the crab alive or dead? He couldn't resist and plucked the tiny plate with the crab in the palm of his hand and turned to asked Jamila. "Is he alive or dead?"

Jamila looking at him from her leaning against the

breakfast table, with her sandwich in hand, stopped chewing and upon hearing the word "dead" swallowed. It bought back memories of earlier this morning. She completely forgot about the dead man as she was taken up with her feelings for Liam. At the same time, Damascus entered the kitchen and starting to laugh. "That's Calypso George. Meya found him and name him after George Takei. She sends out a message to the universe asking to meet a man with the name of George, not like George Takei coz da is askin' too much. Ya know, de Laws of Attraction."

Liam raised an eyebrow and looked at Jamila who began to choke. Damascus seeing her face red and tears running down her cheeks gently pushed Liam out of the way and pulled the trash basket out from under the sink. He pushed it towards Jamila who emptied the somewhat lunch and banana into the bin. Liam had pulled a chair and placed her in it. Damascus handed her the bottle of water he had taken from the hurricane stash and she took a few sips from the bottle.

"I chokkked oooooon mmyyy ssandwiish," she stammered trembling worse than a leaf in Hurricane Iffier.

"What happened that made you do that?" Damascus demanded to know from her. His eyes were concerned and worry etched on his forehead. What was so terrifying? What was bubbling beneath the surface that had Meya choking on her sandwich? He knew it was something threatening, and it was ready to boil over, nonetheless, he kept himself in check.

"No, don't tell him, here," Liam whispered pointing to Jun in the other room and mounting his name. He got up and went into the room to see Jun fast asleep on the sofa. He was about to walk toward where he came and saw Damascus. Worried met demanding eyes and Damascus knew it was serious. He told Liam. "Let's put him in bed." They picked Jun up, took him to bed, and closed the door. Upon hearing this, Jamila took several deep yoga breaths to calm her nervousness. She was beginning to tremble again when Damascus walked in front of her and said to her in a very gentle voice.

"Meya, what did you do to Jun?"

"I puttt aaa sleepin' pill in his waterr sooo he would sleep. We saw a murder, Paxz, we sassssssssaw a murrrrder." She was jittery, trembling, and jumped on her feet as her hands gapped hold of his t-shirt; she began to weep. The fire of rage was burning deep in her black eyes. She was swallowed by rage; rage was an emotion she had experienced before, however, it was never felt so intensified. Damascus held her and rubbed her back as his eyes darted Liam to talk who was standing frozen by the door to the kitchen, looked at the two people in front of him, speechless. He began to tremble with anger and then shock took over and anger entered again. He was not sure why he was angry and to whom. What he does know the one female who means something to him was scared and that scared him too. Irritation about the murder and resentment bubbled until his inside felt on fire. Frustration angrily cut into him and drew small lines around his lips as he tried to gain control to string the words together to express Jamila's and his frustration before her emotions of anger physically surfaced again.

Damascus and Liam knew that Jamila was riding the numbness and fear; fear had a massive place in the equation as it hovered tangentially in the background of her thoughts. The fear of not what is to come; the fear of seeing murder live for the first time. Fear was the cold lump in her throat and that fear in her eyes made a hallowed in his heart and his fear of what is to come burrowed into this stomach. He worked to control the anger that gotten the better of him as Damascus eyed his expression and seeing the various emotions running havoc in him gave him his space.

Liam's frits clenched and unclenched as he tried to gain

control; instead blazing fury engulfed his body. Inkling frustration was fueling his anger which irked him further because for the first time in his life he was at a loss. He reined her fury which distracted him and slipped images into his thought he couldn't afford to have or wanted its visual. Jamila's pain with a combination of the murder and knowing he is responsible became his concerns and made him perfectly lost. More rage pumped through him and short-circuited his brain. He has an avalanche of questions with no answers and that terrified him.

Jamila began to choke again. Damascus pulled her away from him, picked her up, and ran the few feet into her bedroom into her bathroom. He pushed her head gently into the toilet bowl as the last of her lunch gushed from her into the bowl. She straightened up and Damascus flushed the toilet. He held her as she took some water from the tap to wash her mouth. He picked her up and laid her in her unmade bed. He pulled the covers over her and left her. He entered the kitchen and opened the cupboard looking for some painkillers. He found them, took two out, and picked up a bottle of water from the table that she was drinking from and was about to walk when he remembered Liam who was feeling really sorry for this mess he's involved in, however, he's more concern for Meya right now. Murder, damn what the fuck is this? "Here man, you can have some rum." He walked to the cupboard and opened it handing him the bottle. "Come into the room when ya don', will ya?"

Damascus didn't wait for a reply; he hurriedly returned to Jamila and gave her two painkillers with some water. She lay there for a few minutes before she opened her eyes. She forced calm into her voice which by no means she felt. She looked at her friend and whispered softly. "I had to give Jun the sleeping pills because I knew you are home and because the plywood was off, and we had to tell you what we saw. I didn't want Jun to know."

"What did you see?"

"Rest Jamila and I'll tell him." Liam's stern voice nonetheless shaky erupted into the room. Jamila closed her eyes and started to tremble violently. Damascus feeling her energy peeled back the covers and climbed into bed with her. He pulled her to him and held her close. He comforted her. He looked at Liam giving him a nod to start talking. Liam complied, taking sips of rum right out from the bottle. He needed comfort too and a half bottle of rum will have to do.

It took Liam a good fifteen minutes to complete the events of this morning. Damascus making mental notes as to what should be done next and who he should ask from him. Liam is in no position to help them; he had to find a safety net for her. England seemed terrific, however, the boat was badly damaged and the airport is close for a few days. Liam exhaled a deep breath as he completed what happened, leaving out the intimacy between Jamila and him. He is not about to share that with anyone. Jamila can tell him; somehow, he felt she wouldn't do it either.

"Do you think Jun is involved?" Damascus had to know.

"I don't know. I really don't know what the fuck is going on. I'm going to find out one way or the other. Someone is using my company for smuggling. What they are smuggling is beyond me. Jun is a buddy, a mate I trusted with my life. I knew him most of my life." He added in defense on Jun's behalf.

"You're going to have to leave as soon as Jun's up? Jamila is gonna to leave on the next flight out. No, I in not telling you where; it's safe this way. You get this mess clean up and then we can talk again. I trust that you will keep her out of this mess."

"Oh God, yes. I promise you that I will never do anything to bring harm to her. I will leave and return to the yacht." "The engineer is on the yacht. You'll have to be careful when you get back, not to let anyone become suspicious.

In case Jun mentioned you were gone with Jamila let them know you were out in the front yard clearin' the neighba' broke' tree limbs off the garden."

"That's good," replied Liam.

"I think you should leave the yacht here and fly back to wherever.

With the yacht here, you can return with a K9 to investigate what's on the ship. We don't have K9s here coz we don't need them."

"I had a feeling something is hidden on the yacht that Lamburg wants and couldn't find or get to." Liam volunteered his opinion. A thought ran into several others and he voices them all. "Who he killed I don't know him. I'll talk to Captain Hinds about what I saw leaving Jamila out. I think it's the engineer and now with him on the yacht, I don't know. Anything about Jamila I'll leave up to you. You can use your discretion. I leave all of my contact numbers with you. I rather you don't call. Let me do the calling. I'll get a pad and pen to take your info." He concluded and signed depressingly.

Damascus glanced at Jamila and upon hearing her breading, he looked at Liam gesturing him out the room with his head in notion to the door. As Damascus slowly moved Jamila from his body, he slipped out of her bed and followed Liam out the door. He left it half open just in case she becomes hysterical again. He had given her a painkiller and a sleeping pill. She will be awoken later in the day, long after Liam and Jun left. "If the boat stays here and all of you out de island, there is ah good chance that someone is gonna to be fish out of de watta. He's gonna ta screw up big tim'." Damascus informed him.

Liam emptied the bottle of rum and finished the fish sandwich next.

He will need a clear head to manage this mess. They were silent in the kitchen for a good twenty minutes. He was thrilled that Damascus was calm and working with him on his mess. He broke the silence as he put the empty dish and rum bottle into the sink. He glanced at George Takei sitting dead as a doornail looking at him. It hit him then and there about the crab, dead or alive and that set her to remember the dreadful incident. Oh hell, what the fuck did he do to her? He felt her anguish and he shocked violently again.

Damascus saw the color changed in Liam's face and understood some of what he is going through, however, the sooner he leaves the better. Jamila is who he is worried about.

"Don't blame yourself for somethin' you have no control over. It isn't your fault. As soon as you leave, I'll call the police. The telephone and mobile are out. I have a radio to call them on. I go and see where the body is and take care of things here."

"Thank you."

"Tell no one, except the police on board and you've to figure how to do it that's safe. Tell him about the plan and where you and the crew want to go. He will make it happen."

"I am truly grateful. Can I have your contact number? If I can have a paper, I will give you mine."

Damascus glancing at the pad lying on the kitchen counter looked at Liam. Poor man he is a mess, couldn't even remember he left his information his morning before he went out to remove the plywood. He tore a page out of the pad and wrote some numbers down and handed the paper to Liam. "if you lost this you contact Captain Hinds and tell him you want to contact me. When I talk to him, I will tell him I am helping you figure things out."

"Thank you. I'll go pack my things and wait for Jun to be up."

Damascus nodded his dreadlocks head. "I'll go and inflate the raft and see you at the wata edge." With that, he headed to the door the strangers came through a few hours ago. Liam went to his room, made the bed, and lifted his overnight bag up to leave. He was packed and ready to go when he awoke this morning. He didn't want to know Jamila when his yacht was involved with smuggling, well murder now. He went into Jun's room and woke him up. He was out of it. "Time to go, man." Jun nodded a response, tried to get up, and fell back into bed.

"He can't get up right now it will take a good thirty minutes more."

Damascus whispered to Liam from the door. Upon hearing his voice Liam jumped.

"Well, help me put him in the raft. I can inflate it there and you can help push us out to sea." Liam more or less asked Damascus.

Agreeing with Liam's idea, they set about completing the task. They retrieve the raft from the beach and instead of deflating they left it inflated. It took a good fifteen minutes to see the outcome of their work. Jun, however, was half asleep, the drug from the sleeping pills, and clueless as to what took place. Liam had planned to leave him in the raft until he fully woke up; he climbed the ladder into the yacht. He'll have one of the crew babysit him.

Liam waved to Damascus who returned in kind. Damascus was relieved to see him go as now he can focus on Jamila. He has time to get the police and run to the beach to see about the body. He ran back to the house and check in on Jamila. She was fast asleep, slightly snoring. He collected the keys, locked the doors, and ran to the place where Jamila described the murder taken place during her sobbing. He had spoken to his cousin, Clive aboard the yacht with his radio when he went to inflate the yacht. Clive came out on the deck to talk to him and seeing him with the raft waved. Damascus stood standing at the very spot of the murder as he recalled the conversation with Clive.

Captain Peter Lamburg was on board Sincerity drinking and laughing with them. Engineer Xanthippos

Xydis was quiet and pretending to be sick. He knew that his boss and Jun are at the beach house. He also knew that Clive caught him spying on the house this morning through binoculars and saw the murder. What Lamburg was looking for was beyond his knowledge. Unless he was trying to see if the body he murdered was still there. It was not there!

4

The deep indigo tinted on the Caribbean Sea heightened the few trees and shrubs with glittering dewdrops of water from the ocean. The sun has risen as usual and so are all life forms that are inhabited on the tiny island. The sun's rays wavered in and out of the greenery as the white sand changed color from the ocean's spray. Water slammed against the rocks harder and faster than the last ones as the ocean's spray touched the shrubs and bounced back into the sea carrying dead leaves with it. New varieties of birds of various species that were once thought to be extinct either before a meteor strike or volcano eruption darkened the sky and lower to the beach with chitterling chattering voice with some flying squawking a chatter of birds' gossip. Crabs duck for shelter as another round of waves came rolling in on the white sand, splashing with more force against the rocks. High tide can be a rightful bitch thought the crab as he played hide and seek with the aftermath of the ocean's spray.

Breakfast will have to be held back because he can't make a run for it. Being this tiny is no fun on a high tide morning, hopefully, he wouldn't die waiting, as he looked at his partner of three weeks lying dead from starvation. He has to go and look for another lover; he's getting too old for this mating thing. He saw the warm morning sun climbed into a cloudless sky as darkly shadows from the trees hollow the gravelly delta of the hills against the background of sand heating up the day that lay ahead. The sun's light spilled from the coastline of the island where a few trees were old enough to drink enough moisture from the dry sandy soil to maintain their existence and gave some shade to the few inhabitants that occupied it.

The one human inhabitant walked across thorn slabs of volcano rocks to the other side of the island which was more than eight feet wide and twice as long and flat. Most of the shrubs barely came up to her eyes. The empty deserted beach beckoned towards a shipwreck too old to be identified. For any crew to be caught in the hold of a sinking ship is a holy terror and take the romance out from the sea. Upon further investigation, Jamila can't figure how a fishing boat laid arrest on the sunken ship. It does, however, explain the protruding mass that is slightly exposed on the surface now covered with white sand and small rocks building into a small island on its own. It lay some twenty feet from where she presently lives. She can see from the formation a beautiful island is growing and more so two islands merging over the centuries as one. Unless the wrath of hurricanes collided into the small one and push it up again the larger one, thrusting the peak of the little hill that still rises upwards into a mountain.

Under the sea, an abundance of fishes made homes in the hollow
of the decayed ship's structure. Fireflies blinked in the distance vicinity giving guidance to her snorkeling. The saltwater behind her erupted in a patchy angry foam as it fought to move the ship that lies in its path. A lazy water current raged sluice into an overflow of the ship's structure that pointed to the surface making the metal on the opposite side a verdant blur. Intimate knowledge of the limestone character can be learned just by watching the communication between the wreck, the sea life forms, and the water that lay under the sea. Debris of plastic and dries leaves sailed across the sea, landing on a cushion of air while a cool breeze lifted the heat off from the sun.

At night when the moonlight reflected on the ocean and with shimmering water puddles of shadow lay on the surface of the ship's wreckage, some dusky ghosts with ruse special effect materialized from the shadows and they look so real in the faint light of the moon and the imagination of Jamila. She has ghosts for company.

On low tide, there is a stretch of land up the coast behind the tiny hill that is slowly rising into a mountain, where the island bends very low to kiss the depth of the sunken ship which swept through a tunnel and a ravine that rose a few feet above sea level, joining forces with the bottom of the silent volcano resting in the wild of the sea. A few sea birds paused where the ocean water once emptied into the Caribbean Sea that was washed out by centuries of water flowing from hurricanes. One day maybe a half a century from now when she will be old and grey, the two islands will become a massive Barbados, well maybe in a century time.

This early in the morning matched the depth of the joy Jamila is feeling as she indulged in a fantasy of Liam rescuing her from her new home, a hideaway haven from the bungalow in Barbados. She had been here three days and it's getting to her, three days since she last saw Liam, the murder and the murderer. She would recognize him anywhere as she glanced down to the stretch she made of his face. She looked over both her shoulders as if someone, the murder was ears dropping on her thoughts. She shivered lightly and jammed a mental break on her thinking before she gave in to this craziness and idle thoughts of daydreaming versus reality.

She took her snorkel walk to the ship's wreck fishing for breakfast or was it lunch? She lost the measure of time, nonetheless as she dives into the wreck, she mentally wished her small friends a warm hello and eyed the lobster that sat gingerly behind the silver lining of a battered ship's chair. She slowly swam in closer without much of a wave and spared him. She apologized and told the lobster that she has to eat. On land, she lit the grill, Jamila's thoughts unruly drifted back to waking up from sleep in a hellish nightmare and finding Damascus running to her rescue, and Liam is gone without saying goodbye. Damascus holding and feeding her laid her back to sleep. The length of time she has been out of consciousness was two days. Two whole days and nights Damascus nurtured her through shock and back on her feet. He couldn't stop the nightmares, however, as always, he kept her safe.

As she looked around the tiny island where Damascus bought her for safety until he can figure out what happened to the body. The body was gone, disappeared in a few hours and so did Liam and Jun. Appear and disappeared, puffed, just like that, no not like that… appear, kissed, and disappeared. Damascus had asked her "where's your watch. Meya?" Someone was inquiring about a watch he found and would like to return it to the owner. Jamila didn't know where her watch was unless upon her falling on the ground it broke free from her waist. She knew she had it on when she left that fatal morning with Liam, however, where the bloody watch was, was beyond her. She didn't know it was missing until Damascus asked her. The watch is engraved with "love from Kishore," her father had given her mother the watch who had given it to her because her mother rarely wears watches anymore.

"Oh, darling I don't work anymore, I don't need to be on time for anything, besides I have a clock. You take it *beta*. It looks good on your beautiful hand." She wore it on her right hand because she's left-handed. Who was asking for the watch? Where did he get it? He had to have found it on the path that leads to the murder site and Damascus's and her bungalow. This is the only logical explanation, which would mean he's looking for her! Damascus had booked a vacation for his parents and her mother to France. He told them that there's no need to stay in this mess when they can be having fun. There was no need either to worry her mother or his parents with what she saw; the least they know the more likely the murder will be caught. They are out of danger, which leaves Damascus! Damascus had confided with Clive and both decided to get her off the island. While she was sleeping, Damascus's lover Winthrop stayed with her as Damascus and Clive put their plan into action.

Winthrop is British and he was booked for London. Damascus promised to follow him as soon as he saw Jamila to safety. Winthrop knew not to ask any questions because there was something fishy going on. He knew never to get between his lover and his lady friend besides he understood their relationship. Jamila doesn't interfere with their relationship either, however, he does wonder why she's drugged heavily. Damascus would never tell him, and he knew if he asked that would end their relationship. Why ruin a good thing, a very good thing? Darn it, this would make a good tea time gossip.

Clive stole Mr. Ian Bradshaw fishing boat because it was the fastest and he was on vacation in Australia with his family. He wouldn't know since he left Clive in charge of the fishing boat since he grew up with his son, Nelson, and daughter Monica. Clive taking the boat for a spin was not superstitions. Nelson and Clive had given Mr. Bradshaw sleeping pills a few times and stole the boat going on a joy ride with friends parting the night away. Most fishermen go out at night so early the next morning consumers have fresh fish. During the week, they go fishing in the morning, and by afternoon as Bajans go home from work they have fresh fish to cook for dinner. Jamila gave a laughed when she pictured Mr. Bradshaw oversleeping two nights in a row and missed going out to sea to fish. It would be his first two days missed in his life of fishing.

Clive and Damascus didn't purchase anything require for the plan on the desert island for fear it would reach the wrong person. They sailed the one hundred and eleven points three nine miles to Kingston in St Vincent and the Grenadines. They bought can food, fruits, a cooler, a one-burner gas stove, novels, a generator, and a camping tent to set up a temporary house for her on a deserted island between Canouan, Isle Quatre, and Baliceaux Island. By midnight everything was set up for the island trip that would be her new home. They had it all worked out and no one would know that she is leaving the island. It was a great plan. They smuggled her out and bought her in the early hours of the morning as the hidden sun began to show light.

Jamila has been quite happy and more in control of herself. She's safe, however, sad that she didn't get to say 'goodbye" to Liam. Would she ever see him again? Damascus taught it best for Liam and Jun to leave as soon as possible and to get this mess sorted. Jun might be involved. Liam had the promise to keep in touch with him as soon as he can gain some perspective on the smuggling and murder. Damascus didn't want to take the chance of having Jamila in shock and incapacitated, added to that someone is looking for her.

Damascus and Clive waited at the bungalow to see who would come knocking at the door looking for her. Every chance Damascus can spear, he and Clive would visit her bringing supplies and the latest gossip. The radar would pick up a fishing boat leaving and no one would be suspicious that it isn't the owner because the Coast Guard knew of the relationship of Clive and Mr. Bradshaw; besides everyone was too occupied cleaning up the debris of the hurricane.

Who on the island would move the body and where would they put it? Jamila's mood was distant from the norm. One minute she was as happy being by herself with no demands from anyone, enjoying her life, the next, her mood was thoughts of Liam and then back to "where's the body?" These moods are trapdoors and she kept falling into one minute then out the next, however, they were haunting her. She still had her nightmares; only now, it was she they were trying to kill. Every night she had the same dream and each time she woke herself from dreaming, screaming. She hated sleeping. She glanced down at the dress she designed, the last of the lot. Her stretch pad is full of new designs she planned to make as soon as she is off the island. She put it with the other piles of books, picked up her sunblock, and applied a thick layer on her body. She grappled her cap and laid it onto her head. The sunglasses were added and she quickly changed her yellow bikini to a purple one. Bikinis were her clothing for the last two days and nights.

Jamila picked up the binoculars, pulled her length to its full height, and walked a few inches between some trees up the little hill. This is the highest point on this tiny island out of nowhere. Damascus didn't inform her of how he knew about it. She suspected that he and Clive discovered it some time ago in their youth while galivanting and partying. They had a fishing boat and would sneak out in the night with some other teenagers. What they did was never revealed to anyone. There was no evidence of anyone ever being here; somehow, they clean up after themselves. She looked through the binoculars and looked around her to see if she can spot any human activities. Satisfied that there was none, she returned to camp, picked up a bottle of water, and walked to the only set of volcano rocks on the island.

The rocks were still wet from the high tide. She climbed to the highest one, looking for crabs, finding none she sat down on a smooth one. There were ten trees with lots of shrubs to hide her green tent from view. She only used the generator in the night to put the air conditioning to sleep from exhaustion after snorkeling for hours investing the shipwreck and the coral reef that sat a short distance in the Caribbean Sea. She has a battery-operated fan during the day. Damascus had taught everything. She had a funny feeling he did this for himself many times when he wished to be alone. Usually, that seemed whenever he broke up with a lover, he would vanish for a few days. When he returned there is no pain in the past relationship. She too learned to do just that with her few lovers and all broken relationships, looking to understand her contamination or contribution.

One day she and her past lovers quit quenching each other's thirst, and as the sun disappeared and the night settled in, they felt the profound change that has taken place between them. One day the electrified energy died, and the realization surfaced that it was more a physical attraction. It never lasted. There is electrified energy between Jamila and her potential lover Liam, the very same of drinking the same light and breathing the same air. It felt different and more intensified than any other relationship. She smiled; out of nowhere when she wasn't looking, a ray of light return to her heart, sweeping away the empty months of darkness she had experienced; she had mourned the loss of physical attraction and welcome true love. No other male had stirred her as Liam did; they both knew that it's true love. Oh, how unfair!

The heavens collided when she met Liam. She wanted to get horizontal with him again as the beautiful evening streamed. Horizontal with him, hell the morning sun is getting to her. Has he forgotten her already? They are at strange places in their lives and oh, how it felt so perfect, so beautiful. Her poor heart sundered the anguish of leaving something wonderful, something that just began to grow strong, a feeling of true love. Liam, oh Liam, what are you doing now? Her once smiling lips shimmered with passion. She closed her eyes; her head fell back slightly to remember the taste of his lips. She wanted to release her tension on him. She wanted his hot, sexy body, he can quench her thirst. She's hungry for him, oh hell, her heart is beating faster. She gave out a sound that came from within that signal her body aching for him.

Liam heard her calling too, her heartbeat, and kissed her nose. His hands caressed her breast slowly. He stopped and looked at her. He took her hands into his and pulled her up on her feet. He let her rest on his body and the minute her heartbeats subside, he lifted her off from him, turned her back to his chest, and bends her over the seat of the sofa. He softly smacked the right cheek of her bottom and entered her quick and swift, moving in and out of her in a hurry. His manhood requested her presence as she made loud music from deep within her heart. Before she could breathe her next breath, he softy wack her cheeks of her bottom again and empty himself into her. Sitting on the rocks she felt herself creamed after as she felt him made the music of his own. His sound of music sent her into a cascade of emotions as she yelled out his name. An internal orgasm was the cream of the crop for her, however, she'll settle for this external imagination of releasing some sexual tension.

A swarm of seagulls in the distance yelled with joy as they sweep down and scooped breakfast out of the ocean. She jolted out of her dreaming quicker than a bolt of lightning. A crab nibbled at her thigh thinking it is breakfast. She screamed out a loud "ouch" and jumped up looking at the critter. Leaving the rock, she walked around the island for half an hour eventually entering the sea for a swim. She took a quick bath with the freshwater Damascus left to get the salt out of her body. She added aloe-based lotion first followed by suntan lotion, changing into a white bikini, and made breakfast of eggs, toast, and beans. She washed it down with some freshly squeezed orange juice.

Jamila cheered herself up with a mystery romance novel she started last night and soon dozed off. The seagulls were excited about something and she woke in confusion before she rose to her feet, lazily. She took the binoculars and ran down to the edge of the ocean. Her feet touched the warm water and wriggled her toes in it. Looking through the binoculars, she saw some dolphin dancing as the seagulls picked at them. It was a beautiful sight to look at and she was lost spying on them, all playing with each other. Before she knew it, time slipped by and she felt a sting of the sun's ray on her bare skin. She dipped back into her tent and put the fan on, returning to her book. Her stomach growled at her for food. She rolled on her back and lay there for a minute thinking of Liam. She groaned a sound of annoyance and pulled her weight to her feet. She retrieved the fish from the cooler and made herself a sandwich with lettuce, cucumber, tomatoes, onions, Bajan hot sauce, and mayonnaise. She washed it down with a cool iced mauby drink.

Jamila listened to the sound of the earth and it was silent too. A dead silence beholds the island as silent before a storm. Realization slammed into her that something is not the same, not quite in order. Danger lures as time drift by. What type of danger? She questioned and asked simultaneously. She can't fathom a guess as to why it disturbed her. She left the tent behind her and walked around the island. She had forgotten to add more sunblock to her body and felt the sun's ray stinging her flesh including her shades. The walk took five minutes and stopped, glancing at the sky, looking for evidence of a storm brewing. Finding none, she walked to the water edge and wet her feet, listening. The water had receded out and broken shells littered the sand. Suddenly it hit her, even the song of the breeze has a silent rhythm.

Mixed emotions tightened in her chest. The rush of emotions cascaded throughout her body giving into a pounding heart; she never felt the pinnacle of emotions before and they all chewed at the back of her throat. She winded her eye a complicated path from the corner of one side of the island over to where the shipwreck laid to the length of the beach traveling back and forth on the side of the sand and sea. The zig-zag patterns terminated the emotion felt as a sense of somewhat visual relieved her that nothing seen nothing gained.

Whispered cryptic words is her only companion; a frown furrowed her brow in wonderment. Sorting through these flooded of emotions, frustration and worry tore through her as fear rose in her throat. Tempered in the moment of her mixed emotions that surfaced trying to help her understand what she is feeling, she touched her stomach and took three yoga breaths to settle her nerves. Comfortable with her feeling under control, she returned to her tent and started the grill. Worry started to nag at her just as an electric current of worrying traveled through her body. She buried herself in grilling fish for dinner, trying to chase the worry away; it did not, instead, it tightens around her throat.

After lunch or was it dinner Jamila took up reading the novel again. She was highly engrossed with the story; she didn't realize that dusk had silently in her vision. The dusk hasn't come quickly enough for her nor did it lessen the impact of the heat from the sun; the fan did, however, her emotions had settled into worry. In an hour, Damascus and Clive would be here with food, water, a clean bikini, sheets, and towels. She looked forward to their visits each night even if it's only for a couple of hours. She took her camera from its bag and carried it to the beach where a magnificent golden color was in the making of a beautiful sunset. Sometimes, she is in luck to catch a lone seagull or a crab on the beach waiting for something and instead was caught in the water smashing into the rocks. The sea was a wild and demanding mistress upsetting the quiet refuge she had this past few hours. From its crushing embrace of demands, a cool breeze came off the ocean; everything is dead or hiding at high tide and alive at low tide; it seems life forms came out to investigate what the high tide bought in and left for them to sort out for a meal.

Jamila was immersed in the view that she forgot to take the photograph. Something in life is best enjoyed and can't be caught on camera. The sun has rapidly fallen below the horizon and soon shadows will stretch from the shipwreck to the north of the island towards Kingston valley. The mountains will still be washed in sunlight and breeze that was blown earlier till lingered while the cry of the night creatures merging from their home can be heard sharp and clear in the air. Lights will be turned on the islands of Canouan, Isle Quatre, and Baliceaux. Barbados seemed very far away. This is what happened when she lived in the present moment, this is what mattered the most, this very moment is precious.

She ventured back to her tent, lit the lamp, and sat for a while thinking nothing. The lamp burned by itself. Dusk had passed into night and with the warm passing glow, the shadows of the night drifted around the trees as the billowing clouds in the blue sky fell into total darkness. There's no moon tonight, only the brilliance of the ocean and its sea creatures reflected a pale luminescence of eeriness. In the meddling shadows of the night, Jamila crept to the edge of the east side of the island and looked out in the darkness. She felt a spasm of loneliness sprang through her and spread into the darkness below the sea. The lone seagull foot made a rustling noise in the blade of grass next to her tent, too old to fly; she lives there waiting to die. The sound of underground creatures carried by the light breeze into the night air echoed a hollowness that mixed with the shadows of the ghostly figures that emerged from the wreck.

Water lapped rapidly against the shore as cricket chirped noisily and another bird beeped in the distance probably looking for its young. Surrounded by nature usually calm her nerves, however, this darkness that had fallen now wrapped around her resembling a velvet blanket. "I need to burn with you, Liam." Jamila verbalized out loud. "I can feel your anguish and pain; can you feel mine?" The last light of afternoon had slanted from the south and to Jamila's shock the light of the lamp picked out the dead man's face as he fell to the ground. She swished profoundly and lean across to the right and took the light off. She climbed into bed and covered herself.

"I hope when the police surfaced from the hurricane

misery, they would yield something constructive in finding the murder victim." Jamila comforted herself. This loneliness is trigging fear of the unknown. "I no longer like being alone. I want to go home. I call this horrible and stupid. This is a nasty combination of me yielding for Liam and fear of the unknown." This was the frustration felt earlier surfacing as fear, her calm before her storm, the storm of her fears merging with the darkness. She got out of bed and saw a light from a distance. It has to be Damascus. She lit the lamp and took out the gun he had given her and lowered the lamp's light to almost nothing. She picked up the flashlight and waited behind the shrubs. The waft hit the place where she was standing admiring a beautiful sunset a few hours ago. A dog barked and Jamila raise her body from behind the bushes. It was Damascus with Clive's dog, Moonshine. The dog was the ticket for entry, letting her know that it was either Damascus or Clive or both arriving.

"Meya, it 's only I de best lookin' gay stron' back man with dreadlocks lookin' for de pretties' girl in de bloc'." Damascus laughingly yelled out to her. Jamila started to laugh and ran to him. She flashed her light at the load he was fetching on his shoulder and realized that it was freshwater for her to bathe. She turned and gave Clive a hug too. They walked back to the tent and Damascus set the water bottles next to the basin of water outside the tent. He gave her a big hug and held her for a while, rubbing her back. He can feel her fear tonight.

"How's me bes' buddy?"

"I think you know the answer to that question."

"I do," Damascus replied with concern in his voice. "Let's get the rest of stuff, shall we?" It took three trips to bring the supplies into the tent. Damascus took out Baxter's road fish for her with fresh bread and a Banks beer. The three of them sat in silence and had dinner. With the second beer in hand, they went out to sit on the rocks. The crabs are in for the night; the tide is low, there is peace. Damascus broke the silence the minute he saw Jamila sat down. "The guy has not come looking for you yet. He knows it's you and where you live. He's an African man with a heavy accent who spoke to Everton who told Clive." He turned to look at his cousin who raised his bottle in acknowledgment. "Clive and I are waiting for him to come to the house." He took a sip from his beer.

"The police are looking for the missing body. They found blood at the scene and found some evidence there as well. It's being processed as we speak." Clive charmed in. Jamila knew that Everton is a local lad who sold marijuana and grew up with them. She met him several times in her marijuana days.

"Paxz, I think the only way the body disappeared is that it was dumped into a well," Jamila informed him.

"Ya think it's the well next to the Croft's?"

"Could be. Think about it, Paxz. It's the only logical explanation. Someone was paid to clean up de captain's mess. The quickest way is to dump him in the well, washed the blood in the sea, and left the broken branches over the blood. No one would know or see him." Jamila concluded.

"Make sense." Clive supported her statement.

"It's a man that picked him up. I'll tell Captain Hinds." Damascus' black eyes fill with rage when he thought of the murder and murderer. It sent a chain reaction every moment Meya breathe and the killer is at large. He knew this and he is sick with worry for her. "I'm going to have to go soon." He pulled his length to its full height and gave her his hand. She laid her hand in his and allowed him to pull her to her feet. They made their way down to the beach where Moonshine awaits. He let out a few barks, wagging his tail happily. Jamila dropped to her knees and hugged him rubbing his back.

"Meya?" Damascus deep voice fell upon her ear. She recognized his seriousness and rose to her feet.

"Yes, Paxz?" She replied concerned.

"Liam called as he was concerned about you. I catch

him up with the latest. He has his people working with INTERPOL and our police. He's returning to the island to help the police stripped the yacht and see what's being smuggled. He wanted to come and get you and take you back with him to New York."

Jamila knew that INTERPOL is an International Criminal Police Organization (ICPO), which is located in Lyon, France. They supported and assisted all authorities in different countries to prevent and combat international crime. "Oh." Jamila's heart missed a bit then picked up speed, her cheek glowed and she was happy that Liam didn't forget about her also that it was dark and the boys can't see her face although she knew they can hear the high pitch in her voice.

"Do you want to go with him?"

"Yes, is it safe?"

"Yes, Meya, I trust him and you would be safe with him. I think you both should work out your feelings. Should I tell him to come to pick you up?"

"Oh, yes. Please do."

"Okay. He'll have a German Shepard dog called Einstein. Called the dog and he should come running to you. I'll give him your clothes so Einstein will know your scent."

"Oh good." She nodded in understanding.

"I'm not coming tomorrow. I've too much people to help with repairs. You'll be extra careful. Leave the stuff here and take only what you want. Clive and I'll clean d' island after you gon'. Liam will be here in the morning after tomorrow. He'll not come in the night. If anything happens, go by the rocks and wait for him. Make sure he's not followed before you greet him. He should be alone as he is using a friend yacht named "Eris.""

"Okay," Jamila replied taking a deep breath. "Einstein the dog and Eris the yacht." She repeated and stored it in her memory for future usage. Clive stepped forward and hugged her and held her at shoulder length. His hands resting on her shoulders. "Don't worry man, everything's going to be al' rite." He hugged her and whistle to Moonshine who happily jumped into the raft, found his place, and lie down. Damascus gave her a big hug and walked to the waft. Damascus waved and they disappeared in the night toward the fishing boat that awaits them. Jamila stood there as her feet welcome the splash of the waves gently playing with her toes. She listened for the fishing boat engine kicked into life in the distance and the sound disappeared into the blackness of the night before she let out the tension and fear that had rolled into one surfacing as headache. She returned to the tent and had a bath, changed into a green bikini, and zipped the tent door shut. She turned the lamp off and lay in bed, too excited to sleep. She will be seeing Liam soon!

The seventy-five-foot yacht *Eris* rode anchor as a contented sea monster with only one mission in hand: rescue. The black skull with its crossbones painted in basking yellow, green, and black flag flapped in commemoration of the upcoming event and celebration of the hot weather statue the venture of liberation. In the heated sun and beneath the thirty-five-foot yacht's lustrous hull roamed the sapphire blue Caribbean Sea. *Eris* came to a halt way out of sight from the desert island that stood in front of the one Jamila lived these past eight days. Liam stood on deck watching the tiny fragment of land through the binoculars. No sign of life there, nonetheless who would expect life on a tiny desert island? It's passed one in the morning; he has to wait until the first sun's ray to show his face to a new day dawn of a new life with a lady he fell in love with on a stormy night. He suppressed the surge of anger that he had felt at their plight and the no goodbyes. He puffed his cheeks with sadness.

Oh, how he cannot wait to see Jamila. It had been two weeks since he kissed her on that fatal day. Two horrible weeks and every morning he woke up to the sun shining through the porthole, bringing a smile to his heart waiting for this day, the day he will see her, again! Much has happened with the smuggling and murder, he thought of her every chance he had available. She wasn't a lady who inspired anger in anyone contrary, she promoted joy. She took up residence in the center of his brain the day he spied on her on the beach. After they kissed even under the circumstances she surfaced spontaneously as an elegant sensuous lady in the middle of business without knocking first.

Jamila blocked the light from his brain and short-circuited the wiring, the chemical into pure love. He tried to cut her off at the passing hour of midnight, instead, he lay awake thinking of her. He would be happy to supply details, however, he couldn't understand what was wrong with him, his brains and his imagination had only Jamila in his vision.

With Einstein right next to him, his friend's dog whose only home is *Eris,* there was no chance of him sleeping. He patted the dog on the head and seated himself in a chair overlooking the ocean and the vast distance between them, maybe not that vast, fifteen minutes by raft, however, it felt very close yet so far away. He will be right here waiting for the first light to set sail to recuse Jamila. Recuse, who is he kidding, it's the other way around; Jamila recusing him from a life of loneliness and meaningless sex. Liam closed his eyes and leaned his body back in the chair with fingers laced together behind his head; his thoughts drifted to the day he had to leave Jamila and face the hell of the murderer, murder, and smuggling.

In the raft, Jun told him he was poisoned; the Captain cooked the chicken and he believed that he deliberately didn't cook it all the way because he remembered after he had eaten most of it he saw how red it was on the bone and had stopped eating it. A short while after he had a terrible headache and threw up then he had a fever.

The crew had a funny feeling when the Captain volunteer to cook. Jun continued that X knew more than he does because he pretended to be sick so he can get off the yacht. Liam cautioned him to remain quiet and speak to no one about any of it until they are alone and out of sight of the Captain. They boarded his yacht and he headed straight for his cabin to send an e-mail to his friend Simon Shelby who is retired from MI6.

Military Intelligence is British, and they are in charge of the United Kingdom's counter-intelligence and security agency; a part of the intelligence office of the Secret Intelligence Service (SIS or MI6). Jonathan Evans is the Director of the British SIS since 2007. Liam knew that even Simon probably doesn't even know his real name due to too many aliases on covert assignments. He has been retired for some twenty years, however, he has contacts and Liam trusted him, with his life. The smuggling has been going on for some time; for how long and who is involved, he is clueless. After the email was sent he stayed in his cabin until Clive and four other police officers came aboard to escort them to the airport. He was informed that the debris has been removed from the airstrip and American Airlines is the only plane ready for takeoff.

Liam ordered the captain to give the keys of Sincerity to Clive and with that out of the way, he and the crew left his yacht to travel to the airport. He didn't look for either the Captain or Jun nor were they in the car with him. He figured that they were in the other car and on the plane, he sat with his housekeeper Natch, who he knew all of his life. He did, however, meet the eyes of Captain Lamburg that were filled with hate, and a mocking glint entered as they made contact with his; his body reacted with rage. Liam puffed his cheeks in frustration and cold fury formed in his hazel eyes. He didn't want to give anything away particularly that he saw him murdered someone. He had hoped that the Captain would figure he was angry about his yacht being left behind and not the real reason behind his anger.

Two men were left on board his yacht and he rode with Clive and his partner Elston. They informed him that they would like to strip the yacht down to see what is hidden. They believed that there is something on board that Lamburg wanted. Liam told them to wait until he returned as he is going to do his investigation and he wanted some time to arrange it. He wanted to be there when they strip the yacht and see the evidence for himself plus he wanted to videotape the event.

"You want to keep it quiet?" Elson asked him.

"No, confidential because Lamburg doesn't know that Jamila and I witnessed him murdered a man. I want Jamila out of this mess. It's mine and I have a feeling that it's bigger than all of us." He informed Clive who nodded in agreement. Clive informed him not to get in touch with anyone on the island as he would eventually be informed. It's best for the safety of all involved. Liam knew he meant Jamila. He would comply, as he too is worried about her. He told Clive that he will be in touch with Damascus. Clive knew better than to tell him not to because Liam is not a man to take orders from him. Elson briefed him on letting the crew go home and not have much contact with any of them. He also wanted Liam to send Lamburg on some assignment to occupy him for him not to feel suspicious.

What a grotesque situation? Meeting the lady of his dreams and having to leave her in a state of hysterical. He knew if he stayed, she would be in danger of ruthless Lamburg. He probably has others on the island waiting to collect what was smuggled. Seeing her lying there in bed with Damascus holding her shook him terribly. His thoughts shift to her room; painted lilac, closet on both sides of the room with a bath to the right. Simple and define her persona, however, the most surprising of all was her queen size bed with no headboard sitting in the middle of the room looking out at the sea. A palm and coconut trees were standing a little off the foot of the bed. Candles were everywhere and it gave a very warm romantic atmosphere. With Jamila constantly in his thoughts, a deep uneasiness filled his heart. Were they two people seeking release from an indifferent world?

Upon arriving in New York, he told the crew to go home. He ordered his business manager to go to Greece and build him a yacht that wouldn't create problems for him. He didn't want to give Lamburg an assignment. He wanted him followed; he can lead his detectives to this boss. Who is behind this? Who is piggybacking on his business? Sometimes the bruising job as a business leader is a difficult one. Liam remembered some decisions he made over business merges that were the fringe of ersatz ditch diggers and he had made many enemies. Was the destroyer one of them? He doesn't even remember who they were which made it harder for his team of investigators.

For him to have any future with Jamila he had to prepare their future by studying his past. His jaw hardened as he planned a grand scheme of his history to relate to his investigators. All things in his past as well as his family flooded the present moment and as much as he wanted to let it go, to release it, he knew he had to hold on to it until the murder and smuggling came to a conclusion. He hoped that it was not the images of the past only his vivid imagination that haunted this venture into smuggling, leading into murder. Besides if he wanted to know what happened he has to look into the past to see how others had operated and why this mess is happening this time in his life or for how long it was happening that INTERPOL was investigating.

In his apartment, he made several calls. One to his rival in business and asked for a favor, can he please borrow his yacht? His business rival, Adrian Bahar Al-Karachi answered yes because he knew that Liam would never have asked unless it was serious. As much as he's curious, nevertheless, he has his hands full with four wives and ten children. The audience with the cousin of the king had just ended, who merely telling him to control his wives or find another country to live in because his wives are demanding women's rights from him, damn liberation!

The next call was to his family letting them know he wouldn't be coming home this summer as too many things are going on presently and would try to be there after summer. He called his chief pilot and told him to get the jet ready for London. He made the final call to his MI6 friend, Simon. He had lunch with Simon at an out of town restaurant. He doesn't know where he lives and never asked. Anyone watching them would think they are two regular men having early tea, followed by a few drinks and early dinner.

Simon was all excited about doing some investigating. He saw his friend's eyes glittered with anger, the anger that was building during the journey back to his surroundings. He has been old and retired, however, his brain still functions among a few other things he told Liam with a wicked winked smile and a chuckled. This is a piece of cake for him. All he has to do is hack into every secret database to see what he'll come up with and in no time "wolla" the answer to Liam's questions. "Who is framing him or who is using him for smuggling?" Liam had to haul him back to reality a few times as his thoughts wandered to the "good old days." The spying, the booze, and the women, oh yes, the women, Simon wondered if there is any of his seed growing anywhere.

"Are you sure you are in good health to do this?" Liam jolted him back from his wandering into the past.

"Of course, ole man. I am way ahead of you, thinking about what to do and who to contact." Simon lied in his cockney accent noting Liam's quizzical frown.

5

It took a momentary glance, as hazel met black eyes before he closed his and breathe in deep. Instead of gaining control of his senses, he lost it as he inhaled the vision of Jamila. The smell of her sexual scent threatened his life by drowning in the vast ocean of her physique. Time is of no essence as time passed it seemed to overflow into the present moment. She came to him walking on air, smiling as their eyes mated; she unzipped his short and allowed them to fall. Before she could go any further, his hands moved to her hips and turned her around. He pushed her clothing over her waist, discovering to his amazement that she was not wearing any underwear. He entered her from the back in a quick smooth movement, turning them both so the water fell where they joined. He held her in place and pushed in and out as firmly and quickly as he could. He freed his manhood, wait until she said, "oh no" and collapsed into her. One hand was around her waist and the other hand was lock into her hair gentle tugging at it. His lover drenched him and him to her.

"Liam, time to go." Captain Japer Farrakhan said softly touching him on his shoulders. Spooked from his dreaming, Liam's eyes flashed with anger because he was awakened from an exotic dream between him and Jamila. He looked up at the Captain and was about to yell at him when he saw a seagull flew over his head and return to the present moment. He suddenly remembered that he's going to rescue his ladylove. His heart lit up and set his eyes with fire. He pulled his length to his feet and thank Captain Farrakham, heading to his cabin for a shower. In minutes, he was ready and up on deck as the yacht anchored as close as possible to the island. He's sure Jamila can see it. He retrieved the binoculars from where he left them last night and glanced through them. Nothing in sight, not even a single bird.

Liam climbed down into the raft that was set up for him by a crew. Einstein was already awaiting his presence. A little water crept into the raft as he almost lost his balance and leaned too much onto the left side. He is nervous upon seeing Jamila, especially after being awakened from a dream as alive as the one he had of them together in the shower. A cloud passed over the sun and the air grew colder. Sensing the change in the atmosphere, he started the engine as a cool salty breeze blew against his sweaty face.

The air rose and Liam sniffed into it, quenching a distant thirst. The scent of the salty sea air on a pearl white morning heightened the excitement in his heart. Throwing his head back, his hands-on motor, he studied the sky for a long minute, trying to stay in control. This is the age of the dawn on a beautiful summer morning, where the beauty of true love isn't tainted with a fragile string of sweet innocents nor is it intoxicated with visions of abuse, trauma yes, abuse no. It's intoxicated with sunsets, a bird birching, and imagery waterfalls of mystic stolen moments.

Stolen images, not moments Liam thought as he pulled the waft on shore and jumped out upon the beach. His feet touched the warm water and he allowed Einstein out to sniff about. He pulled the waft further into shore and began walking towards the shrubs. As he approached the tent, he saw no sign of Jamila in view; he can hear his heart missed a beat and his breathing picked up speed. Liam refused any open invitation to speculate as to what could have happened. Instead, he returned to the waft. He looked for Einstein and spotted him by the rocks. He began walking towards the cluster of volcano rocks and saw Einstein disappeared from view behind one of them. Damn dog, probably chasing a crab, then he caught his breath and saw her hand on Einstein's head. She pulled herself up and looked at him. He lost it!

A silhouette figure materialized from the short distance decorated in a blue bikini with an orange wrap around her waist. The trick of the light caused by the sun combined with fear created an illusion hardly detected by the eyes. She had slithered into the beach grass and crawl between the rocks frightened as a salamander the moment she saw the outline of the yacht. Goosebumps raised on her skin the size of lizard's eggs. The sun hovering in the sky didn't aid her fear and she felt the sweat on her forehead, between her breasts, and her neck slowly trickling down her spine. Her eyes were red-rimmed from excessive saltwater from her six o'clock swim this morning which didn't relieve her restlessness. She studied him as she emerged from the rocks with very short hair more of a crew cut, mated lips, and bruised cheeks she just received from the rock when she lost her footing and stumped on one. She was too overjoyed from seeing Liam and stumbled; she felt no pain.

Liam couldn't move; he opened his arm and welcome her with a grin that can be felt and be seen in the depth of his eyes. She fell into his arms and inhaled his scent. She looked up at him with trusting loving eyes; with the pads of his thumb, he wiped the tears off her cheek and touched the bruised marks as their lips automatically touched. Liam's broad mounded lips swooped to her dark classical ones, which was open in sensual welcome. The spark of fiery passion exposed itself and he struck on touching her for a moment as the flaming hot energy, flared into a blaze of passion neither Jamila nor Liam had ever experienced before in their life. The thought of her tongue meeting his, created an explosion inside his body. He felt the tan flesh of nipples erected against his chest as tongue meeting tongue sending a vibrant message of love. Hands danced from one hot zone to another, neither caring where it took them, just as long their love can be express.

Consumed by the flame of passion, they became the flame themselves alight with deep sensations of arousal. Stepping closer into each other bodies so that there was absolutely no space between them, his tongue sorted hers in a ritual mating of true love. His chest touched the tips of her breasts as his hips thrust against hers. She returned instinctively passion for passion by using her lips, her hands; her whole body to express her passionate feelings for him and to arouse the same in him. Jamila's body recognized its master as his loins grew pulsing and probing at her feminine entrance. She automatically arched her back trying to embed him within her. Her sensed seized upon his touch as her swelling breasts and tightened nipples send a rush of warmth liquid, dampening her secret lady's core.

Liam broke the mating between them and looked at Jamila, her eyelids lifted as his hazel eyes softening sensuously meeting black eyes. Diamond drops of moisture sparkled at the corners of his eyes and he scooped down and lifted her off her feet into the raft without breaking the connection. The air was highly charged with emotions too fragile to be disturbed and no words were required. It's magical to be whisked away from a desert island. The sensations aroused is beyond the ordinary, beyond the beauty of the many sunsets and the seagulls. Einstein was there waiting for them. Jamila turned and looked at the distance between them and the yacht. She turned back and Liam and grinned. They silently spoke the same message of true love. Einstein glanced at both of them, put his right paw over his eyes, and groaned loud letting them know he knew that love is in the air, however, the noise from the engine deafened his sound and it went unnoticed.

Upon arriving, Anwar, a crewman climbed down the

ladder at the side of the yacht and extended his hand out for Jamila, who gladly gave it to him. Liam observed how she climbed aboard the yacht sexually in her blue bikini and wrap. A sensuous smile touched his lips. Next was Einstein who was put into a basket and hauled upwards to the deck. Liam arrived to see Jamila shaking hands with the crew and giving thanks. He quickly walked to her side, put his arm around her waist, and guided her to his cabin.

Einstein took one look at both of them and decided to follow and see if he was right. Liam guided Jamila into the bathroom and lightly brushed her lips with his and when he spoke his voice shook. "Have a shower or a bath. I am going to see to breakfast and your things being collected from the beach." She had collected her things and put them together in the tent. Captain Farrakhan had inquired about her things and she had told him where they were while she was shaking his hand.

Jamila too shook up to speak herself smiled as she looked into his eyes. She leaned forward and gave him a deep long passionate kiss, answering any questions he may want to ask and don't know how to, and put all questions to rest with a "yes." Liam answered her kiss with a passionate bite jagged kiss he didn't know he had in him. He caught her lower lip between his teeth and pushed her away from him. Jamila giggled as he turned her away from him towards the door to the bathroom. Liam shut the door quickly. He doesn't trust himself with her anymore. He gave himself a shake, took several deep breaths, and left Einstein with her.

Up on deck, he ordered breakfast for both of them, then told Captain Farrakhan straight sailing to New York after he sent two crews to pick up her belongings. The captain informed him that he had already dispatched three crews and as soon as they arrived with the lady's belonging, he will set sail. With no more exchange of communication, Liam headed to the kitchen and took the tray of breakfast from the crew, Lacmina. He thanked her and return to his cabin. He entered his cabin and put the food on the coffee table, drew some food into a bowl for Einstein with fresh water. He headed for the bathroom. Liam hesitated for a few moments upon whether he should wait for Jamila to exist or should he go in and get her. He chose the latter, turned the door's knob, and looked in. She was standing there with a white towel around her, hair blow-dried, looking at him as if she knew he would enter.

Liam swallowed hard and covered the few feet between them, cupped her head between his hands as his thumbs swept across her cheekbones missing the bruised area. He lowered his head for a kiss and this one was surprisingly soft and extremely tender. His mouth barely grazed hers and every time their lips touched, barely yet the touch of his mouth against hers made her ablaze with passion and she melted. Their connection built sensations upon sensations making them intensified. His arms crushed hers to him, molding her to the hard contours of his manly body then suddenly he pushed her away very gently and watched her. Black met hazel eyes and she turned warm and grew damp.

Somewhere in the heat of the moment, the towel was no longer covering Jamila, however, neither of them noticed. Liam's clothes were suddenly off as he reached for her. He cupped her backside and yanked her up to his erection. She crossed her legs behind his back as her arms tightened on his shoulders. She shifted her body angling toward his firmness. They made a loud melody simultaneously as their heartbeats escalated to an all-time high as her soft moist warmth met the hard fire of his and Liam lost control. His heart jackhammered his whole body pounding with pleasure as his lover return touch for touch, kiss for kiss. He moved as swiftly as he can and laid her on the bed.

Jamila welcomed him as he quickly entered her. She lifted her body hands on his shoulders to receive him with a loud symphony of sounds that made his feelings tangible. He provoked her by softly betraying the hardening of her nipples beneath the action of his thumb as it gently squeezed them. His mouth clamped down on the other and he nibbled a little and squeezed the other, heightening the arousal to the point that Jamila fell into the bed and pulled him down upon her.

Taking the hint, Liam moved in and out of her, one minute quick and the next slowly. Jamila unable to take the teasing tightened her hold on his back with her legs and moved her body to his grove. In a few short seconds, she added a different symphony to the already enhanced version of sounds making music. A sunburst flooded his inner being and his hands tickled with warmth and he felt his body tearing within as he beat faster. Liam pulled out from his lover, with his free hand slid under her bottom, and quickly turned her over where he propped her backside to his hips. He made a grinding motion against her and before either of them could breathe another breath, he entered her again.

Jamila grasped in surprise and let out a loud laugh as Liam pushed in and out. He was burning up and as he felt her heat, he became more aroused. He needed to quench his fire that was burning within since he met her. He was the space invader entering a new sanctuary and he loved every minute of it. They made the sounds yet again developing a new symphony of music this time together. The minute he came out of her, he turned on his back and pulled her on top of him. They lay there quietly until their breathing became normal. He bent his head, pulled her hair, and puckered a kiss on her lips. She was almost asleep, and he joined her. Einstein listened to their quiet breading and thought how mistaken he was to assume that it was true love in the air, more than that making love is in the air. Doggone it, now he wanted a lover and it is a long way to New York. With his thoughts together, he knew what he had to do. Get the hell out of this cabin and stay out!

Jamila drifted into a dreamless sleep and came slowly awakened by her stomach making a howling noise. She climbed out of bed looking for food. She entered the next room concluding that it must be in the living room. She looked around her and saw Einstein lying there peeking at her. She blew him a kiss and he came happily to her. She rubbed his head and back. "I am looking for food, Einstein. Know where some are?"As if understanding her, he jumped to the tray sitting behind her then run to the door. Turning, Jamila saw the tray and looked for Einstein, she let him out and returned to the food.

Liam turned and stretched his arm out to put around Jamila and it fell on the bed. He opened his eyes and saw no one there. He looked at the bathroom door and saw no lights on. He quickly jolted up and ran into the next room. He halted as the sight he saw was amusing. Jamila was naked eating cold eggs and toast. He noticed his share was also gone and so was the cold coffee. Suddenly ecstasy entered his heart and he wanted to tug on her nipple with his teeth. He wanted to slide into her again to feel her heat and to see her come apart in his arms. He wanted to move in with her. He wanted his firm traction to enter her now!

Liam was so focused on her; he didn't realize that he too was naked and standing tall, erected. Jamila glanced up quickly and grinned admirably at the sexy image on display for her."Have you eaten all, my sweet love?" He teased undauntedly as he lifted her from her seat to his hips.

"Yes," Jamila admitted running her tongue over her lips tasting the last of the cold coffee and eggs. She rested her hands on either side of his muscular shoulders eyeing him, daring him to make the next move.

"Oh, good." He said lightly. "I have something in store for you that will definitely fill you." He grinned at her never breaking the eye connection as he walked to the bed and lay her gently in it. Some time into the late afternoon, Liam slowly glided his hand over Jamila shaped of her hip; then let it slip down to her lady's core and lingered there for a minute before he began testing the waters of her moistness. She felt a rush of dampness gushing out of her at his contact. She is fully awakened and realized it was not a dream. He was preparing her body again for the act of his love!

She can feel his manhood webbed just above her backside. Catching him off guard she suddenly moved from her side; gently pushed him onto his back and climbed aboard. She bent her knees and sank them to his side, pinning him motionless. She embedded him to the hilt in the tight warmth core and he completely filled her. A gasp of surprised contentment escaped her when he flexed his backside and obligatory himself, even more, deeper into the chalice of her body. He whacked her one cheek of her backside. He lifted the other hand into the notch of her core and stroked her into a sensational bliss as she rocked back and forth, making music. The rhythm and tempo escalated to a breathless pace until they both climax at the same time. He laughed heartily overcome beyond bliss.

Two weeks later with one-stop for refueling and spending a few days in the United States Virgin Island of St. Thomas, they arrived in New York. The rainfall was so heavy as they approached and at times the Manhattan skyline almost disappeared from view. They saw thunder rumbling in the distance and a streak of lightning sliced through the blackened sky. They had sailed in the Caribbean Sea and into the Atlantic Ocean onwards to New York. The 174-ft. yacht was made in Italy and doesn't require refueling. Liam wanted to spend some time with Jamila, he had instructed the Captain to make one stop for food and to sail slow. This was the first time they will be alone as his instincts told him of danger in the very near future.

Liam and Jamila enjoyed the cool cascade of drops

as the zephyr came off the bay tousled their hair. They ran into the cabin for shelter not too soon as a jolt of lightning came with a crack of thunder banishing the faint shadows of the city. In the wake of the rain that seemed to stop dead for a moment then again let loose an extra bucketful before stopping for good. He was content with whatever was sent; the weather did not bother him or the spring or the harsh winter. This mess did and as worried as he was for his love's life he knew that he now has the strength to pull through anything. Jamila was with him.

The yacht docked at Crescent Boat Club Inc., a private marina in Clifton Park, New York. Liam hailed a taxi and together they headed for the penthouse located on Fifth Avenue, two buildings into East Thirty-Second Street. The building of the penthouse stood small from the ground looking up. Amongst the cluster of building it looks old with its rustic physique; not where a penthouse would usually be in New York. Jamila was exhausted to care much and spoken little on the way to the penthouse. Liam was on the mobile phone speaking to his people in various languages about business. She understands the French and English part of it, however, she was a total loss when he started to speak different African languages. They had spent two weeks together on the yacht, Jamila lost count of times they made love. They watched the ocean's life through telescopes and binoculars exchanging information as a migration of birds and sea life danced on to a new destination. She told him of her life on the tiny island, the ghosts, and the shipwrecks. The crew was not around as they respected their privacy.

She had spoken to Damascus and he promised he would visit her as soon as possible. Their parents are having a ball of a time. They didn't speak of anything else. Now here she is with Liam in New York City heading to his home. She is overwhelmed by how her life has changed upon meeting him. She promised to spend some time on her own as soon as her feet touch the ground. In the meantime, Liam was on the mobile phone talking to a member of his board and she noticed the tiredness on his true love's face. He promised that he would give her some time alone, which would be hard since he can't keep his hands off of her nor she with him. Suddenly, a concept hit him and he decided that they would travel around the world until this business is taken care of and they can be all alone without looking over their shoulders.

Liam has the most trusted person in his life working on the smuggling and the results would be theirs soon. Simon hasn't called him since they met in London. At least this smuggling and murder mystery had bits of visible evidence, therefore there has to be a trail somehow, a paper trail, and a murder trial. He has a thousand theories of what it's all about, however, he didn't arrive where he is in life presently by theories and speculation. Liam wanted evidence. Simon will unravel it, he's the best there is in uncovering secrets and solving the mystery. He finished his conversation on the mobile phone, reached out, and pulled her against his chest, her backside on his legs and against his stomach, settling his head above hers. She leaned in him relaxed as they melted into one. He held her there until they arrived at his penthouse. Liam heard Jamila's intake of breath and struggled for his breath. They both had a rude awakening of love and life. He loved how she reacted to his simplest touch. It's time to face reality; he can take the next step with her and they can be a couple. For now, he has to protect her and himself; he can't make any promises that he'll have to break. Being lovers is killing him; he wants to make their union a permanent one.

The Indian taxi driver, Raji pretended not to notice either of them at the back of his vehicle. Lovers will always do what lovers wanted to do, regardless of the place and time. He was too glad to pull up at the curb and left them with their overnight bags and headed out for another pickup. Liam had instructed the crew for their luggage to be left on board as they would be returning in a few days. Damascus did a good job of packing Jamila some clothes and personal things that lay next to him on *Eris.* He had watched Jamila's cheeks turned to a bright pick when she discovered where her clothes were and with whose, more so someone when shopping for her. It was the natural thing to do; to put their belonging together, it made sense.

The elevator rocketed to the top floor faster than speedy Gonzalez. In the elevator to his penthouse, Liam's hands had reached down locking her fingers under his lips. In response, she pressed her tights against his and felt the fierceness of his passion with the same urgency that she is experiencing, rising from her body. She felt her heart hammering, keeping time with his heart. She arched her back as Liam's lips moved down her throat to the open cleavage moving through the fabric of her dress to the swollen mound beneath. At this time, as she took him into a world of making love, there is no question of either of them resisting, as they can feel each other sexual passion rising and driving them into an instant shattering crescendo of passion that tore shuddering sound from her throat. In the moment of passion, their kissing sends tension in their faces, the flush suffusing from their skin. The elevator stopped at the floor and they reluctantly tear themselves apart and stepped out. As they entered the penthouse, Jamila was aware that some luggage was there awaiting their arrival.

"What are those?" She asked in surprise.

"I had my assistant buy you some clothes. See what you want and take the suitcase; when we return to the yacht you have your own." He said softly brushing a kiss on her lips.

"Where are we sleeping?" Was her next question; he pointed towards the direction of the master room to his right unable to speak. Jamila followed his finger, turned to him, and blew him a kiss. As she walked in the direction of the master room, she took her jacket off and tossed it onto a chair followed by her shoes, blouse, and that were the last of her undressing that Liam caught before she disappeared from his view. Jamila adjusted the balance between hot and cold tap and allow the stream from the water to run directly into her face and hair. She tilted her head back against the tiled wall, opened her mouth, allow water to splash against her lips and teeth. She moved under the spray of water and turned the water to a little more cold than warm. She was there less than two minutes before she felt a strong arm drew her closer to her lover's body. They stayed there for a long while enjoying each other as well as the water falling upon them sends a cascade of rippling sensation throughout their body.

Liam's fingers skimmed over the flesh of her breast with both hands. They were flushed with arousal as he cupped both running his thumb over her brown nipples. She leaned back enjoying the sensation of his seduction. He pushed her breast up, pulled her back, and watched the waterfall on them. Unable to take any more he turned her around and took a turn with each center of her breast between his lips. He grazed them with his teeth and played with them with his tongue. The intensity of the pressure from his seduction elicits a ripple of sensation with enough finesse to tantalize the owner's nipples as he drew taut; he continued to brush it with the tip of his tongue.

Unable to take the tingling sensations from head to toe, Jamila lowered herself on her knees to his manhood and took all of him into her mouth. The shock of the change took him by surprise and the arousal of lukewarm water and very warm mouth send him into orbit into ecstasy. Enough was enough for Liam, he bend his knees and reached down to the back of her thigh and caught her backside and Jamila realizing the change of command let him go and rise to the occasion. She dug her nails deeper into the hard muscle of his shoulder as her body directed him insider of her. He thrust against her hips as his hands hold her backside firm and she contracted. He thrust more passionately a few more times as the waterfalls where they joined. They both came simultaneously.

In the days that followed Liam was occupied with sorting out the mess he found himself involved in when his yacht landed in Barbados. He had set up a credit card and money available for Jamila who went shopping. He assigned a bodyguard with her permission who followed her under-covered. Many times she turned around to see if he was there and didn't see him, however, she knew he was and was thrilled that he was discrete. She went along with her ventures pretending to be free, enjoying New York and what it had to offer, and visiting the old places she loved on precious holidays. This day she returned as usual in time for tea only to find Liam furious. She was halfway to the kitchen with her package when he exploded with rage. She wasn't aware of his presence until he yelled at her. Apparently, he was waiting for her and couldn't, it seem waited to express himself. She put the package down looking at him refusing to move or go to him.

"Where the hell were you? I have been worried sick? Why didn't you leave a note?" Liam snapped with anger, his mouth clamped in tight and dancing in his eyes a hard gleam of rage which kept flickering for a few seconds before it shifted in shades of dark hazel if it is possible to ice water. Anger had his jaw firming, his breathing heavy, telegraphing all the way up the bluff, tightening his ribcage, and the few scotches he had waiting for her return burned right through his anger.

Jamila's eyebrow rose in puzzlement and paranoia renewed its ugly head, anger flashed in the normally calm eyes. The burst of anger drove her back against the wall in shock holding on to the packages. On her features, the flush of anger that lurked there didn't hide the fear that swept into her feelings. Anger wasn't her main emotion fear was, however, being yelled at made her edged into anger, and wanted to shout at him for yelling at her. "I understand the depth of your anger." In the first display of anger, she managed to say softly and quietly that Liam had to lean forward to hear her. The possibility that someone is looking for her and wanted her dead had anger roaring through him. He fritted his teeth at the surge of anger that went through his body again. His eyes narrowed in anger as he looked at her and his angry gazed zeroed in similar to a laser ripping her heart open.

Anger filled the air and in the square of this anger silence lingered as the truth that lay dormant slowly showed its face. Something had replaced the love of a few days to this anger, what? A new burst of fear rushed through her entire body and she began to shake. Jamila's hesitation to enter the room set off another burst of anger inside him. "Liam, you don't have to yell. It will not help this anger between us." She said shakily and with annoyance. She angrily wiped away a tear with her shoulders. He saw in her eyes a mirror of the same emotions that are coursing deep inside him. Surprisingly his voice was low, however, it trembled with the emotion of fear and anxiety.

"I have to yell because it helps release some of this anger I am feeling, otherwise I'll have to throw or break something." Sharpness entered his tone however the anger had dispensed to his surprise. No one had the courage to openly confront him about the stress he was under and it was probably for the best because he was seething with mixed emotions that were waiting to erupt quicker than a volcano. The jab of anger he felt was replaced with a tinge of fear. The coil of mixed emotions then attend to spill forth curbing his anger, anxiety wined in turning his thought in various directions and his anger grew again. He bit back his angry retort that was irrelevant upon seeing the tear she wiped away. She should be angry at the twist of life that took her away from her friends, family, and home. Why isn't she angry? He wondered.

As much as anger and fear burned in him he saw her distraught expression changed to angry speculation of what is this all about. He wished he knew. Hiding his distress behind anger caught his attention and he realized it was fear that he was operating from and deep breathing to gain access to control. Even in his anger, he recognized his truth. Liam clenched his jaw tighter at the thought of losing Jamila. Just the thought of what happened to the man that was murder injected a firestorm of anger rushing through his body. This anger was inside him since that fatal day and kept swirling, taking him into stages of what it turned out to be present. His feelings were numbed from fear however the tsunami of angst shifted into fear which now melted down to stress. Seeing the tears that were quickly replacing her fear, he melted the anger, the fear, and replaced it with his love for her. He moved quickly and pulled her into his arms standing there for a very long time pulling on each other strength to calm their bodies. As soon as normality was returned and Jamila felt it she can speak with him she lifted her head that was resting on his chest.

"I have always told you where I go personally or leave you a note. I did leave you a note on your computer as usual. I had my mobile with me you could have called." Her voice was a bit shaky, however, soft and understanding. "I told Charles." She concluded.

"You did. He must have forgotten to mention it to me. There was no note and I forgot about the cell." He looked at her for reassurance and forgiveness. "I am sorry I truly am. I don't know what that was about. I have never done anything close to that. I never had a reason to be angry. The mere thought of losing you ....."

"Shhh, just hold me." She didn't want him to finish and held his hand and gently pulled him into the living room where he was standing a while ago. She pushed him into the sofa and sat on him holding him. He picked her up and slide onto his back and pulled her on top of him holding her.

A week later, Jamila stood frozen listening to the butler, Charles on the phone. At first, she couldn't comprehend why her body was frozen as she watched him prepare coffee for her and Liam. She was at a distance and couldn't understand what he was whispering into the mobile phone and whom he was talking to except that it was brogue. Her instinct kicked in high as she watched him took a small long colored bottle out of his pocket and poured the content into the kettle. He took his mobile phone off indicating that the conversation was over and put it into his pocket.

Jamila felt that this was going to be pleasant to confront Liam about his faithful butler. She became suspicious of him after her note to Liam disappeared and he didn't mention to Liam where she was going and doing. She kept an eye on him and told Liam that she wanted to cook the meals for them so she can stay occupied. She took a deep breath and called for Charles. Her voice was surprisingly calm.

"Yes, I am in the kitchen making coffee," Charles answered.

"Oh, I will take it in. How long more for the toast?" Jamila asked upon reaching the kitchen.

"Oh take the coffee and I will bring the toast. Oh, I know you too don't want to be disturbed, I will knock twice and leave it by the door." Charles turned to give her the coffee tray. "I have errands to do, I will be off for an hour or two." He didn't give her eye contact and kept his back to her. His voice was empty and vague. Jamila gave him eye contact, however, he didn't rise to the bait. Son of a bitch, you bastard, what the fuck do you think we are fools? She smiled at him and he heard a different sound he was not acquainted with her voice.

"If you don't mind since it is Sunday I would like to visit a friend for lunch and possibly stay for the night." Charles gave her a bright smile and a wink indicating a possible sexual liaison. His smile, however, didn't reach his sad green eyes that showed the wrinkles of some seventy years. His once straight broad shoulders drooped an inch or two forward and his lean body showed bones paced to white freckled skin. Sadness overshadowed his features. Jamila watched the kaleidoscope of emotions raced across his prominent bony nose leaving his cheeks pink. He was operating from a purely emotional level. His words were simple, however, they were laced with intense emotions that cracked his feeble voice, and raw pain radiated from his eyes.

Emotion chewed up the back of her throat and she swallowed intensively around the tightness hoping to sound excited. "Of course, and thank you so much for making me feel comfortable and all you do for me." With that said, Jamila took the coffee tray from him and left the kitchen. The smile left her lips the minute she was at safe distance. Charles watched her vanished into the master room. The toast popped up, added butter, cut two slices of cheese, and added it to another tray. He covered it with a towel and followed Jamila's path. He refused to think, afraid that they would hear his thoughts. He knocked on the door twice, lowered the tray upon the table by the door, and left.

As he was closing the front door, he let out his breath and felt sorry that he had to do what he did. Someone wanted them dead and they held his lover, Mavis hostage. He showed them that he was adding the liquid to the coffee as requested on the mobile phone they had delivered to him. He had removed all of his money and personal things including his lover's and had them posted to his friend in a different country. He is taking Mavis and leaving for good. He had given service to his master Liam for twenty years, however, it is now too dangerous. He deliberately knew that Jamila would catch him as she usually picked up the coffee at that particular time.

Liam had a feeling that Jamila saw Charles put the poison into the coffee and he threw the empty container into the trash. He had deliberately taken the note and refused to convey any messages to Liam for her as he usually did. He wanted her to be suspicious of him because he knew Liam trust him with his life. He had gloves on, hopefully, the police will find the killer or someone's fingerprint or at least the mastermind behind this all. Liam would know how to find him when he wished to if he wished that is to find him at all. Charles walked out of the building and slipped the killer's mobile phone into his pocket. Within minutes, his mobile rang and he heard his lover's voice. He told her where to go and wait for him there.

In the master room, Jamila related the incident to Liam who picked up his mobile from the nightstand next to the bed. He was about to make a call when he stopped and whispered to her to go put the shower on and packed her things together. He believed the flat might be bugged. He pulled his body out of bed, added underwear, a t-shirt, and jeans to his naked length. He told Jamila to wear jeans and a t-shirt with comfortable shoes as he packed his necessity in his overnight bag. He opened the door and looked to see if anyone was there, finding no one, he went into the kitchen and retrieved the empty bottle with a paper towel and put it into a zipper-lock bag. With them both ready he took an exit that Jamila never saw before and they entered East Thirty-Third Street. Liam looked at Jamila and said, "Someone wanted to kill us and Charles knows you saw him."

"No, he he he how?" It was Liam's people and who's she to argue with him?

"He knows your timing and knows you would be coming to get coffee, he hoped you'll see and tell me. Someone is blackmailing him. I have to get someone to look at this bottle. Did you dump the coffee out?"

"Yes, I did." She took a deep breath and said with her Bajan accent deeper than normal. This usually happened when she doesn't have control and fear stepped into her life.

"Don't be nervous. We are taking this way out; no one will see us. By the time they figured anything out, we'll be safe. I have a plan, don't worry about anything. We are leaving through a very private exit, the housekeepers." Liam informed her.

"No worries." She replied in a very nervous tone.

"I have to get a paid mobile and used mine less. Don't use yours, turn it off. As soon as we are safe you can call Damascus and your mother, just in case it hits the newspaper." Jamila nodded too confused to talk.

They left the building and walked a block towards Grand Central Terminal and the Grand Hyatt Hotel. He thought of booking into the hotel while he formulates a plan and figure if someone is following them they would be an easy target. Instead, Liam hails a Taxi on East Forty Second Street. He instructed the driver to stop at the nearest public phone. The taxi driver pulled over on the next block and Liam made a quick call to his rival. Upon returning, he ordered the driver to drive around until he says otherwise. The Indian driver looked through his rearview mirror at the hysterical grotesque creatures in the back of his cab. Rich bitches who leave a little tip and who think they own the world. He glanced again and came in contact with Jamila's eyes. She smiled as if she read his thoughts. Fuck, an Indian gal with a white mmm black or both man!

The body of an old man with a white shirt and black slap laid in the dirt, still. How long he laid there is beyond the owner's knowledge. He stirred slowly and lifted his head from the brownish soil and looked around him seeing fuzzy images. He closed his eyes as his tired body cracked in places he never knew that it could only for a very brief moment; suddenly filled with high-speed energy he lifted his torso inches off the ground. He was on his knees and his arm supported by his weight. "Where the fuck am I? God damn it!" he spoke out loud and panic lined his face. He racked his memory for previous images, finding none he slowly pulled himself upright. He looked right, then left, and seeing nothing he looked up and the bright sun blinded him. Now he is fuzzy and blinded; he saw nothing. He closed his eyes, removed the glasses from his nose, and wiped it with his shirt. He slipped it back on the bridge of his nose and looked around.

"Oh, God, God damn this hell," escape his lips. "What the fucking…bloody hell am I?" He said with contempt as a hard-line crossed his lips and blue eyes darkened with regret. His reaction was one of anger because he thought he could still do the job and now he had to admit defeat, and that he's too old for spying. Simon's cockney accent protruded more than ever. If only he could remember what happened and how the fuck he has gotten here; if he knew where he is, he can find his way out of the mess he has gotten himself into hundreds of times. Being angry isn't a place he wanted to start making decisions because he knew from experiences that it wouldn't work. If only his head didn't hurt this much and his memory could return which he knew it wouldn't due to the age fact and damage done on the previous expedition. Why do people like to hit him on the head is beyond his wildest imagination and his imagination is wild. A wicked smile obtruded from his lips.

Simon didn't move from the spot he had raised; he slowly and deliberately looked around. Anticipation mingled forming volatile aggression into anger. His brain paralyzed from something as he tried to figure the curve of the outline in front of him, remembering and not being able to connect with it. He felt more alert, an edge over his thinking, he did think he still had the zang over his aching body. The blackness that had laid doormat for so many years now exploded in his brain. A small part of his battered brain felt active while other parts told him that it is dangerous to admit that it is dead. Etched in rejection his thoughts fragmented, his feelings numb and his soul frozen in despair, Simon fought back a sign of frustration and irritation streaked through him.

Broad-shouldered felled backward and wide full lips smacked in annoyance as a gray band on his retreating forehead filled with dirt fell on the stubborn jut in his chin. He wiped away the dirt leaving more dirt from his hand. He didn't feel in control as he struggled to remember one shred of information that would set him loose and not cut into him of this predicament he found himself in. He lay back down and suddenly jumped up with the desire to exclude his stomach contents; he did in seconds. A strange lopsided grin stretched on his mouth as the alcohol eroded his defense and a sober expression appeared. He listened to the sketchy details and mistakes his thought bought forth and he allowed himself the grace of finding peace in the vague images. At least it isn't all brain loss and a broader smile craved into the dirty face.

"Ah, yes booze it was so, it shall be." He coiled sobering. Judging by the silence of the day and the strengthening heat of the sun that scorched the land, it was noon. The sun comforted the land that lay barren from the lack of rain. The hot dry summer wind blew the dry dirt onto him as he inhaled he took some into his mouth and swallowed. He started to spit it out cursing the earth for giving him its ungodly sin. Thirsty and aggravated, he looked around trying to figure which path to go right or left. He knew he been here before, however, he cannot remember when and where or for what reason except it was work-related, and with a wicked smile he had the pleasure. He doesn't remember with whom, however, the tingling sensations in his body knew he did and lots of it, endless pleasure.

With renewing interest he allowed himself to look around the dry sun-heated space. Majestic hills rubble came to haunt his imagination. He picked up some stones and silently asked "Where did the stones come from, the hills in the distance? What lies so steep, deep in the hills between this range and the one in the distant? Something is there. What is it? A cascade of recollection drew his memory in full force as if it was yesterday's sunrise. A cloud covered the noise that had been pouring in steadily from the distance gushing down the deserted desolated path and flooded the landing with waves of sounds that tapped into his ears and lapped at his neck.

Simon took his glasses off and put them into his pocket. He lay down back on the dirt road and pretended to be dead. In about twenty minutes, someone will pick him up and put him onto the floor of his vehicle. They spoke Arabic and Simon still couldn't tell where he was, however, he knew that he should stay still as possible. A white man in a land of mountains is not good and he doesn't know who saved him and for what purpose. A half an hour later, someone picked his head up and put something to his mouth. He felt water slid down his throat. He pretended not to drink, nonetheless, after a few tries, he moved his mouth and swallowed. A young boy spoke and Simon was clueless as to what he saying.

He drank some more water and the boy put him down again. A man who Simon assumed was his father spoke to the boy and Simon opened his eyes enough to look at them and his gaze bounded off the men. There was another one staring ahead and another driving the truck. Terrorists!?

Simon wondered what mess he has gotten himself into that put him in this isolated place. His memory still has not fully returned and his body ached all over. He closed his eyes and racked his thoughts as to where he could be and why it felt very familiar. As the truck came to a halt, he opened his eyes and saw nothing except the blue sky, white clouds and felt the unbearable heat of the sun. Two men pulled him out by the arms and legs, putting him to stand on his feet; he pretended and buckled his knee. Hands from both sides of his body held him in place; they half dragged his body into a tent and ordered someone for something.

He was laid on a piece of fabric with something of a soft nature and a pillow under his head. Someone lifted him from behind and another put spicy food into his mouth followed by water. They did this four or five more times and Simon was laid down again. "What I need is some scotch straight up," he thought. Well, maybe no liquor as he believed that was what got him into this mess, expel from civilization. Simon opened his eyes and looked around the tent. He has quickly gotten up and ran to the opening to see what is outside. He glanced right, in front then left. What he saw sent him into a tailspin. He wouldn't speak for fear of being heard. He held his breath and realized that what he thought were hills were mountains. Memory flooded quickly sending him into a spinning wheel of shock. He was in some mountain terrain in Afghanistan, but where? If he could figure that out the dialect, he would know and he can make his way out of here. He's too old for this job. He owned Liam big and this is paying him back.

The sun was slowly fallen below the horizon and he can see the outline of a mountain about the tenths that lie below. Shadows stretched from the mountain to the west end of the valley. The mountains were still washed in sunlight and the slight breeze that had blown earlier currently mixed with the mountain appearance. Fresh air came from the top of the mountains terrain teased his nose as if it was sea breeze. The warm smell of spicy food lifted the breeze and sent it into the animals in the distance. He can hear the low bellow from cows mixed with other sounds of an animal as sharp as if he was standing near.

Simon decided in the early night that he would make his way out of this as he returned to his earlier position on the bedded floor. He has to stay awake and remember to be half-dead. They will return with more food and water soon. The water he needs to store and food he will eat. His thoughts returned to Liam and the day they met. He screwed up his assignment and that was when he knew he was getting too old for his spying job and he should retire. He was tracking the United States Air Force to see how they transport the cargo when some prostitute approached him and of course, he went with her. It was a set up because she drugged him and some men broke many bones in his body, he lost count. They put him into Liam's plane heading into Japan because no one would suspect; Liam would be blamed if he was caught. How he has gotten to Japan was still a mystery. He doesn't even remember how his bones were broken and for what purpose. What he remembered was fucking a prostitute in Malaysia who was spilling her guts out about smuggling and the next thing he knew he woke up in Japan on a plane. Liam heard him in the luggage moaning and groaning. He was in excessive pain and was truly screaming according to Liam, who was afraid to touch him, therefore made him comfortable with some scotch and he fell asleep.

As soon as the plane landed in London, he was patched up by a private doctor. Liam took care of him and saw him back on his feet without any questions. He was off the grid for over two years and no one knew where he was, not even MI6 headquarters. Liam gave him money to rent his flat and leave him to figure things out. Every so often about six times a year, they would meet and have a long dinner. Simon still lived in the flat that Liam pays for and is clueless about where he lived, his memory had many questions and blank with vague images. The money is automatically deposited into his account and goes directly to the renter.

Liam continued to deposit money into his account and still care for him. He lost some memory from the beating, even his original name. He had many passports with different identities and lost his original name. Can he find his birth certificate? Liam called him Simon and that is what he answered to everyone. After he surfaced, he called a number he did remember and retired from "the firm." He asked to have the identity of Simon Joseph Willis aged eighty, a wee bit younger than his eighty-four as his new identity. He was given documents and the address of his apartment in London which he sold. The same date of birth was on his journals he had written over the years. Why he had put his date of birth on his entire journal is a mystery. There is a massive black hole in his memory making him a walking time bomb of disaster.

Coming back to reality as a woman dress in black entered with a man, Simon was fed and was given water three more times before day fell into night. He listened to the sounds of animals and heard no human voice, rose to his feet, planning his escape before he stepped into the night. Thinking about his escape, he put his body on alert and spinning his thoughts into action. Simon Joseph Willis waited until he saw the moon ducking behind a mass of clouds which dimmed the shadows around the compound and mostly along the path that crept to the edge where the animals were penned. Moving by the light of the moon, he followed the smell of spicy food and went into that tent. He took a piece of fabric out and filled some Indian Nan with some other spicy stuff he had earlier. He filled a bottle with water, drank some, and headed out the tent looking for a vehicle, instead, he came in contact with an object, a post that stood between tents.

What is a post doing in the middle of a dessert? Simon thought how peculiar, however, if he had to look up he would have seen that it was a palm tree typically found in the desert. If Simon had his memory he would have known that there was no reason to escape because the villagers knew him well. in fact, they owed him their lives since he warned them that the United States of America was going to rocket them to death in two days. This was during the war on terror and as the world knew there were no terrorists as the United States claimed they wanted a war and Afghanistan was the chosen one along with Iraq. As the world also knew many of the American soldiers were attacking and killing innocent Afghanis. Simon knew this and had warned many of them over the years as he was living there in between jobs. Of course, none of this he remembered and he escaped in the night.

Simon lost perspective for a few minutes as he tried to grasped control of his body, however, when he opened his eyes he realized that the hit to his head unlocked a gateway to his vision of his past. Simultaneously, a fire leaped into his veins as the moon came out briefly from behind a cloud, igniting feelings too strong to suppress and he wanted them to remain dormant and unacknowledged thus he can concentrate on his escape. The feelings, however, had their journey sending a jolt through his body and landed at a very susceptible body part he thought was impotent.

Memories surfaced as denial isn't working anymore. This was a place it seemed that freshened the memory, not erased it. Images came to Simon rapidly, sharp and clear.

Two images particularly flashed in his thoughts; one was his naked body moving on top of a brunette woman and the other was him standing naked in front of the blond one. These two thoughts slid off each other as if they were oil and water and left him in no way understanding the associations. Names popped up Lilou and Nora and two females' voices yelling, 'That bitch Liz told you that Simon is sleeping with me."

"You called her a bitch, are you bitch," was the response. "Oh, no I am not as big one as you, darlin'."

"Still jealous Lilou that he dumped you for me?"

"Oh no that's not jealousy, bitch it's anger."

"You're still carrying anger after all these years."

Simon had a funny feeling it started with two women fighting over him and changed to another topic altogether. He doesn't care, what he wanted to know was why is he under a bed and whose bed it is, the blond or the brunette? He shook his head several times to stop the images. He wanted them to surface when he can look at them, not now when he is trying to escape. Moonlight reflected off the path to the animals as the pale silver moon glowed in the sky, his thoughts figured taking a horse instead of a vehicle. He needed time to be long gone before anyone realized that he is missing. He saw no one, not even the males that transported him here. He walked away from the tent and saw camels. He went for it and as he approached the stock, he realized that the camels were cows. The hit on the head made his vision blurred just what he didn't need right now.

"God damn it!" He untied one and mounted it. He didn't even look back as he rode off. The moon in this terrain greeted the red planet and cast a faint reddish shadow lining the path. A pale silver moon glowed in the sky bending just enough light for Simon and his new friend to track without tripping over rocks and old tree roots. Using the moon as a map, he rode south for a while to a terrain where he knew well. He had marked this place several years prior to his retirement. He also marked where the sunset when he was in the tent with the black goat hair. He looked and felt the moon behind looking on too shedding light when needed and as he came nearer to his markers a flood of memories submerged him. His brain is working just when he needed it the most, "what a bloody relieved" He thought out loud. He stopped the cow and walked to a dry plant next to a rock. He pushed the rock over and found what he had left there, a gun, map, money, an Arabic and English dictionary with a flashlight. His lips curled into a smile, a very wide smile.

He took it all and mounted the cow again heading into town a few miles ahead. He knew where he was because of the food he tasted. Only one tribe cooked this food, and it was the Tajiks, who speak Dari Persian language. He was safe so finally, he asked the question. "So why the fuck am I running?"All Simon knew was that the images bought a hot eruption of anger because his thoughts and fear usually buried him and he usually drowned them out with liquor. Being an agent he's used to living with a cold eruption of fear because of the thing he had done professionally, however, the anger and fear combined are from what he did personally. He couldn't remember much of either life and wanting to be secretive about things that he no longer can relate to or felt connected to was immiscible to him.

The anger subsided and fear was replaced with the desire of a known nature. All he can comprehend from his erection is that it gave his body heat. He was grateful to the ladies for finding the keys to his imagination never mind he does not know who they are he can run with both of them in his bed. Although they were arguing they were warm enough that he can image proximity the intensity of their anger to know he bedded them both. "I was under the bed for Christ's sake." He yelled out to the wide-open space and saw the cow's head lifted in wonderment as his gaze combined to chase off the chill that ran into Simon's spine. He rubbed his hand over the cow's neck. "Not you wonder boy." A thought spurred out from somewhere and he corrected himself, "or girl," patting the cow's neck again and feeling assured that the cow is not spooked.

As the images surrounding the memories cleared he was again under the bed haunted by the memories of making love to the ladies. A simple thought broke free from the chaotic jumble in Simon's head. He shook his head to free them only to stir an avalanche of thoughts. Since he had the control, he permitted them to flow free from where ever they were stored. The brunette lady had shaken his thought mentally to restart it while the blond had mentally shaken him to restart his thought in a different direction altogether. An asteroid of thoughts suddenly bombard him and they spun a web of images of him making love to women all over the world. A kaleidoscope of emotion flooded his body and his head did summer sault pulling him from exotic thoughts and images he never knew could have existed. Simon pushed a smile onto his parched lips and nodded a "yes" so big the whole world can hear.

Adrian Bahar Al-Karachi with black curly hair that matched Liam's affixed his friend with piercing deep-set jet black eyes. His lean and wiry face with gray at the temples supported by muscular shoulders with a light stoop expressed well-muscled arms and legs through the black silk tailored suit. His olive skin on his face showed his lean pointed nose and wiry mouth. Perspiration glistened on his blow and his forehead folded with several lines from frowning and deep in thought. A vein throbbed on the side of his neck and his pulse rate rocketed up a few beats due to the late-night of putting the few pieces of the mess his friend and his lady are deeply involved in these past weeks. He walked around in the manager's office of his hotel where he had promised to meet Liam. They were rivals in business only, however, they were friends first since college days. They met in college and made a bet of who would be the richest. They are tied presently, though they go back and forth now and again with one or the other being the riches. It was a game and a good laugh whenever they met for drinks.

Adrian didn't bargain to meet his lady friend. What an Indian beauty, nice olive skin, beautiful large eyes, and well-shaped all over. They are in love he can tell and she's involved in this mess with his friend is in somehow. He doesn't want to know because that would mean he has to tell his wives. They can get any secret out of him, they know how and Liam doesn't need that presence in his life. The fury coiled in his stomach and take shape of a snake awaiting the correct moment to strike. He was furious that things had come to thus far and at a standstill and he felt frustrated. He was cold and fought back a sign of frustration they wouldn't see it standing in him. He took a deep breath; working to keep the touch of frustration out of his voice that matched the firm grim in his eyes.

"Mavis dates Charles and she was missing for a week. My people finally figured it out when they reunited. Who was trying to kill you, my friend?" Adrian informed and then asked him.

"What?" Liam asked.

"Your butler is having sex with one of my maids, Mavis; guess you didn't know that, did you, George, huh?"

Jamila sat up straighter in the chair when he called Liam, George. She relaxed again as this isn't the time to ask about names. It felt strange to hear his friend addressing her lover as George.

"I'm afraid I have no information about the people's sex life that works for either of us." Liam grimaced with no accent and perfect English.

"One of your shortcomings, my friend; if you didn't have any shortcomings you would've known that someone is setting you up. From the looks of things, it sounds revengeful. George, who would want to take revenge on a sweet sexy man like you," Adrian said sarcastically giving him full eye contact and continues. "I don't know whether they put the two of you together. What I know is that someone wants to kill you for revenge and Jamila because they think she saw the murder. They found your watch and wanted you dead. I don't know whether Lamburg put a hit on you or he told his boss and the boss put a hit on you. My people along with Clyde's and Nyles's are checking into it. Someone wants you both dead, who?" He finished and let out a breath.

"I wish I knew the answer to that question, Bahar."

"What can I do to help?"

"Bahar I need to sell everything to you, all of my business and I want you to have it," Liam said to his friend so serious that Adrian rose from his seat and leaned across the table between them and touch his forehead.

"Just checking to see if you are crazy, guess not. Okay, I will buy it all. Consider it done."

"I want your people to check out the fingerprints on this bottle and see want was inside it." Liam gave him the bottle Charles threw into the trash bin.

Adrian looked at him and said, "Oh, fuck man what've you got yourself into? No, don't tell me. Used whatever you have to, you know where everything is and know how to get it." He lifted himself out of the seat and headed out through the door of the office.

"What do you want for the business?" Adrian asked over his shoulders. Liam quickly followed him and answered his back. "Whatever you want it for, it's yours. The sooner the better and Bahar used your own people." Granted in agreement, they shook hands and hugged with a nodded to Jamila. With that, Adrian disappeared into the lobby through the hotel door into his awaiting limousine. Liam watched the vehicle disappeared into the night. He picked up the phone and spoke French to Adrian Bahar Al-Karachi number one businessman Miklos Nordquist.

"Je suis prêt à partir." I am ready to leave Liam informed him. His fury was deposited and banked deep beneath old debris of past anger. He had to control it until they were safe.

Four of his friends had a code that they had agreed on and only the head of their businessman knew. Clyde Zegaran, Jun Fujioka, and Nyles Gilchrist knew the code. Clyde and Nyles have their people helping Adrian's people investing this mess of his and Jun is lying low in a destination unknown to him. Clyde put him in hiding along with the other crew except for the Captain who Nyles's people are investigating and shadowing. This pack was made a long time ago when they decided to outrun the other in business. Clyde and Nyles are richer than Adrian and him as they invested in commercial airliners and shipping together. They were released from the deal a long time ago, however, they all remained partners as friends until they die.

In minutes Liam ushered Jamila into a taxi headed to the airport. He pulled the cell phone out of his pocket and made a call to the pilot of Clyde's plan. In minutes, the taxi pulled up in a private airport and Liam paid the man, took their two light bags out of the trunk and onto the aircraft. He was in a vast hurry to get out of New York and as he passed the adjacent phone he told the pilot in French, "Je suis prêt à partir." Liam returned the phone to its receiver and to his seat next to Jamila who was seated, buckled her into her seat, and did the same for himself. He folded the table in front of her that she had pulled down to rest her handbag and it disappeared into a pocket of the jet. He reached over, held her hands, and laid his head back. Eyes closed he felt the jet-moving ready for take-off.

Jamila followed suit as she remembered that Adrian called Liam George. She tugged at his hands and Liam's opened his warm hazel eyes and looked at her slightly moving his head.

"Adrian called you George, why?" she asked.

"Liam George Nwosu at your service, my sweet lady."

"What? Are you serious?"

Thinking that she discovered his last name is African, Liam volunteered information about his heritage. "My great-great-great granny Tilly was black and so was her husband. My grandmother and mother are white and my grandmother's husband was half black and half white while my father is white and of Spanish heritage. My grandmother thought if she married a white man she can break the racism and life would be easier, however, she fell in love with my grandfather. I used to agree with her until recently."

"Oh, sweethear' I would be a fool if I think there was no black blood in your genes. Your hair is too dark and curly for you to be pure white." Jamila informed him.

"Oh," Liam looked puzzled at her as he lifted his head and turn his upper body to face her.

"I was talking about the name George." She told him.

"My name is George, yes," looking at her puzzled.

"Let me explain. You remembered the crab in my kitchen you had in your palm?"

"Yes. George Takei?" Liam laughed and looked at her puzzling.

"Yes, his name is not George Takei. It's only George. I found the crab in a mussel while I was washing them for dinner. I pulled it out and wished upon it, hoping it would bring me a sweet loving man in my life. I heard something on the television about George Takei saying something and I named the crab Calypso George then boil the name down to just plain George. I sent out a wish to the universe to send a man whose name is George, to me." Jamila finished and looked at Liam very seriously. Liam was laughing out loud that upon seeing how serious the love of his life as he tried to stop. It didn't work and he continued to for another minute before he started to apologize to her.

"No need to apologize because a man with the name George turned up at my door in the middle of the night of a hurricane." She informed him. Liam laugher went dead as he looked at her very seriously. He didn't know what to think or say.

"Ah-ha, look who's serious? I'm with you and right in the middle of smuggling and murder and have incredible sex and fuck a whole lot of traveling as people tried to kill us. I should've asked for a George without...out this much action."

Liam was lost for words. All that came out of his lips were, "I am so sorry for all of this, Jamila. I wished I never gotten you mixed up in any of it. I hope you will forgive me. I love you with all of my heart and I hate this situation more than ever."

Jamila upon hearing his declaration of love forgave him instantly. "I love you too Liam George."

"It's Liam George Nwosu, Nwosu not George Takei." He couldn't help smiling at her.

She smiled back at him and pulled his head to hers. She planted a kiss on his lips and said, "we will pull through this and after we'll... we'll find a nice quiet house in the mountains and live there. We'll make love and have babies, two babies." She averred.

"With George Takei watching over us?" Liam said matter of fact with a wide grin and glint in his warm hazel eyes that made his eyes twinkled.

"You aren't going to stop teasing me huh?"

Liam realized that the jet was in midair cruising, he loosened their seat belts, stood up, and pulled her to her feet.

"Come let's start making babies."

"What the fu'."

He led the way into a private room and closed the door. It resembled a tearoom and office in one. Jamila didn't have time to look around as Liam slid his hands onto her erotic zones. Jamila raised her hips slightly to accommodate him. She was wet beyond her wildest imagination as he slipped his fingers inside her warmth. He sent his fingers deep into her and withdrew them using the ball of his middle finger to lightly brush that sensitive spot, the killer zone. His thumb idly swayed back and forth across the tip of her gem, while he planted a kiss on her mouth and stroked her stomach with his tongue as his fingers slid in and out of her core. The pressure of the sensation rushed to her heart as music floated out from within her body.

Liam idly moved his thumb and replaced it with his tongue. Jamila lost it. She yelled out, clutched a handful of his hair, tilting her hips upward towards the heat of his avid mouth towards the swirling magic of his tongue. He lifted his head after she climaxed into his mouth. Strands of hair clung to her cheeks and fell into her mouth. He lifted them out and laid them behind her ear. "You are the only lady I cannot wait to make love to every minute I'm not sleeping and when I sleep I dream about you."

Jamila half heard him. Her hands still clutched his hair as she tried to bring her breath to normal. Liam watched her loving every minute of it. He waited until she was almost normal and her hands released his hair. Acting on impulse, he unzipped himself and lifted his erected penis out of his slacks, tumbling into her hands, and without thinking, she lowered her lips to take all of him into her mouth. He leaned back against the bridge and his head fell back. His hand was now tangled in her hair as her mouth warm and wet over the length of him. With a final touch from the tip of her tongue, feathering light kisses on the tip of his manhood, he pushed hotter and quicker for a few minutes. He let go into her mouth. He watched her swallow. Liam kissed her.

Liam and Jamila were two days into the French flat in Saint Germain des Pres when the glass was shattered. Jamila was standing in front, facing the window sorting out the laundry with the maid, Claudine who was attending to the dry cleaning. Claudine, petite squared high cheekbones with a small button nose was backing the window a few feet away from Jamila. Liam was on the phone trying to reach Simon between the two ladies in a diagonal position of a triangular shape, where Simon is at the top and the two ladies are situated at the bottom of the triangle at opposite sides. He had moved slightly to the table reaching for pen and pad while Jamila had walked to the bedroom to put the clothes away, Claudine took her spot, putting the dry cleaning on the chair, removing the plastic bag over the dry cleaning when the bullet struck her.

Liam flung his body towards the wooden floor, yelling for Jamila to do the same in English and to Claudine in French. All was silent for a very long minute. Liam rose from his spot with a feral cry of rage, pulled himself up on all fours, making his way to Jamila who was doing the same, however, still in shock she went down on her knees instead of rising upon them. Liam reached down, caught her by the elbows, and helped her to her feet away from the window. Remembering Claudine, he pushed Jamila to sit on the arm of the chair further yet from the view of the shattered window. He turned to Claudine who didn't move from where she fell. He crawled over, shook her shoulders, and saw the blood pouring out from above her left breast. He automatically put his hands over the spot adding pressure hoping to save her, however, she was dying.

Upon hearing the police siren in the distance, Liam told Jamila to get their bags that were packed. He turned to see if there were any exposed windows and being content that the draperies were drawn on the others, he whispered to Claudine. "*Pardonne, Pardonne, Je suis très désolé. Je vous promets que vos enfants sont bien et que rien ne se passera. Merci beaucoup pour tout.*" In English, it meant "I am so sorry. I am so sorry. I promise I will see that your children are well taken care of and no harm comes to them. Thank you for everything." He heard her last breath, a smile tugged at her lips and she was gone. He closed her eyes and let her go. He went to the sink in the second bedroom nearest to the door and washed the blood off from his hands.

Pugnacious jut off from his jaw; he didn't have time to analyzed his anger which was coming from his body as a sour smell. Ice with rage and mounting with frustration coupled with deep regret snarled his stomach into a tight knot. This anger that seemed fresh, however, was a decade old; memories from a long-forgotten incident came adrift into images of the past, his great-great-great granny Tilly's past. He cannot go there at this moment, he concentrated his anger on getting them out before the police arrived.

Jamila stood with bags in her hands as she witnessed the exchange. She wondered why Liam was sorry and why he promised to take care of her children. She concluded that he probably knew her, therefore he's familiar with her. She was trembling earlier; presently she is numb and scared and frightened. Anger and disbelief flared inside her, twisted a spiral of fear as her instinct kicked, sending her adrenaline to rock high. The hair on her back of her neck vibrated in a rise as she felt the spiral of fear twisted in her stomach. The sharpness in her voice was bought on by fear, anger, and panic, she was shaking. She shook her head managing to speak around a painful knot in her throat.

"Liam...," her voice sounded different and not of her own. It was a mere whisper of fear, a hint of sheer anger and something else, what, she didn't know, yet. The frisson of fear she had felt after the storm in Barbados was nothing compared to the dread she now felt. Jamila stared at the blank space in front of her, turn to Liam as he approached her, his lips pursed in anger. The smile she loved was gone replaced by masked rage as his eyes were black while his face had lost its glow and the pinkish color was red with fear.

"We have to go. I'll leave the door open for the police. I don't want to talk to them. They'll figure it out. My phone?" Liam asked looking around for it. He spotted it where he was lying and went to retrieve it. He listened to see if anyone were on the receiver end and found none, put the mobile in his back pocket of his black slacks. He walked back to Jamila, took the bags from her, and said without eye contact. "Follow me." Whoever heard the shot called the police, he doesn't care. They took the stairs down to the streets and left the apartment complex as the police were arriving. They didn't look at the police nor did they look back. They acted as if they knew nothing of why the police were here. Liam turned the corner and hailed a taxi. They entered it and he said into the driver, Ritz, *s'il vous plait."* He pulled Jamila in his arms and neither spoke.

Upon arriving at the Ritz Hotel, he paid the driver and allowed the door attendant to get a potter for their luggage. He's trembling and doesn't want Jamila to know of his fear because he felt her trembling. He walked with her in his arms straight to the bar and ordered two drinks, Bacardi and coke for Jamila. He needed double scotch. He looked around for an empty table, finding one in the corner that guided Jamila there, sitting her down. Liam was about to take the chair next to her when a man approached the table. He looked at Liam without saying a word, recognizing the man as the manager he walked towards him who left and Liam followed him to the door.

Jamila watched the silent exchange and saw that Liam has a full view of her. She smiled, nevertheless, a smile she knew didn't reach her eyes. He was serious as he listened to the manager. He nodded and stretched out his hand whereupon a key was placed in it. The manager left and Liam returned to take his place beside his ladylove. She waited until Liam finished his drinks and looked at him. Liam understood her looked said, "Pierre, the manager told me that the room that we are going to sleep in tonight is bugged. No, Jamila, the flat was not mine or the room is not either. I didn't take us to my flat for fear they would find us. The flat is a friend of mine, Mannatu, and this hotel room, too. I thought we would be safe there and now Interpol has the room bugged. Mannatu is in some kind of trouble and I don't know what. He knew I was there with you, maybe the bullet was meant for him and not me. We are of the same background, built, and height. I have a funny feeling he's mixed up in all of his somehow. I thought we were over the past and at this time I am not sure." He drained his drink and sank into his thoughts.

She frowned as she sipped her drink. Their world seemed eclipsed in all directions and all of the horizons are a deep blackness. It is the awful inescapable stenches of the toxic poisoning with the brief glimpse of swirling conspiracy of innocent carnage that have overloaded her emotions. Liam said to her, "we have to be careful what we are talking about. Not any mention about anything except sex. in fact, we should give them a good fucking show." Jamila looked at her lover and turned her eyes to the ceiling above her.

The waiter came took their orders as Liam ordered more drinks and some appetizers. Jamila was still hanging on to her drink than actually drinking it.

"I tried calling Simon and couldn't get through. I will send him a text about where to reach us. We are going to a mountain chateau in Switzerland for a while. It belongs to Adrian. Do you want to tell Damascus to join us there?"

Jamila still in shock over the last hour nodded. Realizing her emotional position Liam continued, "Do you want me to send him a text?" She nodded again and sipped her drink. He pulled his mobile from his back pocket and was about to text a message to Simon when Jamila laid a hand over the mobile. She asked as Liam looked up. "Is yourrrr mobillee bugged?"

"No, it's not mine, the mobile is Adrian's."

"How can you take care of Claudine, do yyoouu kkknow her?"

Liam raised an eyebrow and asked, "You speak French? Mmmm Mannatu grew up with her and she takes care of his flat. I knew her for a long time through Mannatu. We all used each other flats whenever we are visiting that country and the flat is free. Our staff knows the arrangements and we do not have to call our friends up for permission. Mannatu has that apartment for his family and he keeps this room in the hotel for his lovers."

"I thought you don't know your employers. You don't have time for them." Jamila inquired.

"I know my employers who I see on a regular basis. I had picked Charles myself. I don't know their sex life as Adrian does. He had them all investigated from time to time."

Jamila contented with the answers nodded her head. The waiter arrived with an assortment of appetizers and laid them on the table. The smell of the food made both realized how hungry they are and they began eating. Liam was talking as he put some stuffed mushrooms on his plate.

"Someone knows our whereabouts and wants us killed. They found out that we were staying somewhere else which means that they are surveying my homes and where I go. They must have traced your watch and knows you are with me. The bullet was a single shot and the shooter thought Claudine was you or saw you standing there fired and you moved while the bullet was traveling and Claudine got hit. The shooter figured I was going to go and see what happened and they would have taken me out too. I didn't and when they heard the police they left."

Jamila nodded. Liam continued, "someone who heard the shot call the police, or the police was probably nearby ad heard the shots. We are going to stay here for a while and when we go up to our room, we shower and pretend to go to sleep." She agreed with a nod. Liam sent the text messages and a few more for Clyde's jet to be ready for takeoff in the morning.

Simon heard the shot and knew that someone is trying to kill them. He figured he would wait around for a call again and receiving none he called the airport for a flight to New York. He was at the airport in Japan when he received a text from Liam. He read the message that they are alive and to meet in Switzerland. He booked his flight and went to the bar for a drink. This flight will leave in the morning. He might as well bunk here at the airport, as he doesn't want to miss it. He ordered a cup of tea and settled into a chair for some dinner. After ordering steak and potatoes, he went over his notes, and not understanding any of them, he put them away. His eyes again, not doing what it suppose to do, read. How can he solve this mystery, help Liam, and his ladylove when his body isn't cooperating? Someone is using Liam's yachts, jets, and business for smuggling. The board is involved in every transaction because their signature is all over the damn place including Liam's or it had to be someone who is forging papers to look like the board of his business and Liam's. That's it. What does the United States Air Force have to do with it and the Triads, KPA, Afghanistan, cocaine, painting, heroin all have to do with this mess of Liam's? What does it have to do with his friend, Mannatu? Unless, someone hated him so much that they are taking him down, for what?

Simon breathed out several times and just when he was going to open his notes again, the waiter arrived and laid his meal out on the table. He eyed the waiter and asked him, "No female waitress, huh? The waiter bowed, smile, and left. "Bloody fucking hell, a guy can't have any fun in his old age. It's all the gay guys serving you. I can't have too much bloody drink coz I would get drunk and forget where I am or worse wake up in the bloody jungle, mmm forest....God damn it... the bloody dessert. I have to eat my food and have nothing to look at except gay guys. Where are all the nic' lookin' straight ladies thes' days." He whispered to himself aloud, looking around him.

He chocked at who was looking at him smiling. He took a sipped from his cup of tea and burned his mouth. The tea spilled on the very spot where his penis laid and he burned that too! He yelled, "God damn it bloody hell," he was tapping the fabric of his trousers and he yelled some more "fucking craze daises," on the discoveries that his penis was fully alive and kicking. As if that's not good enough, the person that he was smiling at said, "Can I join......help you?" in the most beautiful sexy voice. She is a Japanese hooker all right and she wanted him for dessert!

7

The French police that was surveying the hotel room of Mannatu's were in a rightful mess. They had just joined the French Police Force and had this boring job of listening to endless nothing, absolute nothing. At this particular time, they sat in astonishment as the pair of police listened to the racket coming for the room they are babysitting.

"Harder darlin' harder, harder. Spank me harder, harder. Ahh Ahh yes harder, Ohhhhhhh yes, yes, yes, that's good, hooooooo no, no, no, don't pull out. Don't tease me. I can't take it. oh oui, oui plus fort difficile. O vous êtes si bon, and subsequently, it went on for another half an hour with the sexual racket; young officer Ange Rioux swore "fuck" as he looked down at the wetness from his pre-ejaculation pouring to the surface of his uniform pants. Ange name meant angel and right now he is no angel. Eloi Posson, the other officer was taken up with the sexual noise that his zipper was down and his hand was stroking his penis in an up motion. He groaned into ejaculation at the same time as his partner. After a good half of an hour, they look at each other and then at the mess their ejaculation created.

"Ne dis rien. Ce n'est jamais arrive?" Officer Posson asked his partner who replied, "I no say nothing. This neva happen," he crossed his hand while the other covered his wet pants. "Je dois changer mon pantalon." With this agreement, they were about to shake hands and realized where their hands were prior, instead shook their heads. Officer Rioux rose to his feet, took his overnight bag holding it in front of him, and without a word, headed for the bathroom underground outside the parked surveillance van.

Jamila and Liam were on the flight to Geneva early the next day. They were laughing all the way to the airport about the little play they put on for the French police. The mobile rang bringing them to a halt as Liam answered it. She turned to look out the window as the town car zoomed past the Eiffel Tower. She had spent a good six months learning French and touring the whole of France after she graduated from university. She wanted to work for the United Nations as a translator, however, she changed careers when her friend, Nadia was shot and killed while working in Darfur.

"That was my mother, Beulah who called Adrian. Mannatu is at my parents' home asking for me. Adrian said that Mum said that she doesn't know where I am. She wants to know how come he has my mobile and I said I don't know. Well, Mum said when she asked him he told her that I left it at this office two weeks ago. Mannatu is waiting for me to call him; he can express the phone to me. Adrian said that my mother spoke in Arabic, which she never does to anyone except with my father. She speaks our native language to me and everyone else. Mannatu never goes to my house, somehow he is mixed up in all this mess, how I don't know. He probably gambled all of his money and wanted me to bail him out." Liam finished.

"Mmmm him showing up at your home is a treat?" Jamila asked matter of factly.

"No, blackmail, and yes that he can hurt my family if I don't contact him or give him what he wants." Liam finished for her. "I'm going to remain silent and let Adrian take care of it."

"Oh, hell Liam this is getting worse by the minut'."

"Adrian will go and get them and take them somewhere safe," Liam told her.

"How do you know he would do that, I mean Adrian?" Jamila wanted to know.

"About 10 years ago, someone kidnaped one of his sons and he turned to me for help. He used my money, my jets, and my homes to stash his family for safety. It worked out and he had the kidnappers killed. After that, we made a bond to put money away for an emergency and would be there for each other including Jun, Nyles, and Clyde. I have been using that money and their things. We know how to get the money and things we put aside for an emergency. I can't go and get it, they can. I text Nyles for more money and he added it to the card and we are using Clyde's jet. They are all pooling their investigation together and reporting to Adrian who is the key contact man."

"I guess you too are not so much of a rival after all," Jamila said.

"Only in business." Liam mused. "Adrian would have one of his people put money in the safe for us when we get to his chateau. We'll be safe there as that chateau is in his sister Ana's married name and cannot be traced to him. No one knows except Ana and me."

"Oh, good Liam, Simon, and Jaxz will meet us there and we can relax and feel safe. I hop' he found out who the murderer is and the fallen victim." Jamila let out a breath sounding more of a semi-depression.

They arrived at Charles de Gaulle and aboard the private jet of Clyde's heading to Kloten Airport in Zurich then by train to Adrian's chateau D'amour in Vaud. It's safe this way and if anyone is following them, they would be lost. The train rolled into small towns and stopped to exchange passengers as they left and others climbed into the carriages, mostly family with a few children traveling to various destinations. If they felt uncomfortable they can easily be off at one of the stops and take another train. Liam bought tickets to Domodossola with a stop in Bern where they would get on and take a train to Vaud. They would shop for clothing for this time of year where the temperature can dip into forty-eight degrees Fahrenheit for early August.

It would be a long while before anyone discovered where they are staying, more hiding. He had Adrian's corporate lawyer Jin to meet them at the chateau for him to sign the papers over for the sale of his corporation. He felt confident that it will work. Adrian will slowly sell little by little to over corporation for a huge profit; no one will be the wiser. Jamila and he can have some time to work through the shock and enjoy their relationship without looking over their shoulders. He was beyond angry and he knew that when he is angry he is proficient at hitting out at anything with a great deal of force. He needed to get this energy of rage out of his system while he is at the chateau.

Liam leaned over, pulled Jamila to him, and planted a kiss on her lips. "I love you with all my heart. I have never loved someone as I love you. I have never been this afraid for our lives as I am now. I wanted to leave you with Adrian where you will be safe. I can't do it. I need you near me. I want to see your face every morning when I wake up. I keep putting your life in danger all for my selfish reasons." He finished with half of an apology and the other half out of desperate need. The fire of passion added sparks as if it had been lit inside him. She knew from her own eyes that the same would be reflecting the frisson of passion that raced along her spine as his hand caressed her chin raise the level of fire burning inside her heart to an all-time high.

Liam brushed his lips lightly over hers again. He gave a soft infectious smile that she melted. Understanding is going through her thoughts while knowing his love was accessed through her heart which did a less than ladylike somersault. It lit the fire of passion deep within her essence as the light kissing overrode all the anger from the mess they are in, along with her basic common sense. Her sexy black eyes sparked a flame of excitement in him and he wanted to explore her right there. It wasn't the appropriate time they need to heal first. He saw anxiety crossed her face and alarm widening her eyes which slowly warmth sparked in them. He heard her heart hammered loudly as the realization of his declaration of his love was a razor-sharp slice into her core. He had risen to peek in his heart and suddenly it crashed into his ribs stealing his breath away, only momentarily. A mustang-wild pulse beat in his throat ad his heart was awakened to love for the very first time in his life.

Liam reached up and tunneled his fingers through her short glossy black hair as emotion cracked into his voice that is raw with pain. Jamila's cool skin heated from his touch. He turned to her and whispered in her ear, "I am hopelessly in love with you and I want us to be together for the rest of our lives." His warm touch sizzled against her hot skin and radiated in her eyes as his words pierced her heart with passion. Jamila's hand reached out, gave his hand a squeeze, and smiled at him. They cultivated strength from each other and she understood it. She will let him know as soon as this shock and numbness are worked through that she loved him too. There is no other place she rather is than right here with him.

She held his hands until they arrived at the train station. She held on to it as soon as they were settled into their cabin. She turned to the window and leaned against his shoulders as he read the newspaper he had purchased after having dinner. Her magazines rest in the pocket of her overnight luggage. Golden shafts of light beamed through the window in the cabin in the train, creating a warm glow. In the rosy light, everything thing seemed healthy and normal however Jamila knew differently and watch the last light streamed over the mountains. In this shifting pattern of shadows and dim light, lured dangerous animals waiting to feast on a life form for dinner. As the last ray of light slipped behind the tree line her eyes closed and she was in a dreamless world. In the first wash of daylight steamed over a different mountain, she was awakened. The light lifted the mist off the sage of the trees. She studied him. Liam was reading the Wall Street journey still holding her hand. He had not slept. The night had robbed the hazel color from his gaze and seal rage in his body. She can feel his energy of deep-rooted anger burning through him into her hands.

It was going to be another amazing morning erasing all of the uneasiness of the past weeks; the morning clear and unsophisticated, new day dawn hopefully, with answers. This cocoon of darkness on these lovely last days of summer cast a numb spell over her. She can't wait for a new awakening of appetite for life, love, and spiritual innovation, and the appearance of some fresh motivation to live life and not just survive. She knew somehow with her little interaction in this smuggling and murder business they were involved with was a direct action in helping to stem the tide of anxiety between them. As long as what really mattered stayed top priority in honor and they are together without being an easy target for bullets, it will be acceptable to be with him and to love him. Her eyes flashed with fire and the sunrise made her sweat as she remembered the Hell she lived since she met Liam. They are at a sharp angle in the mess that continued to rail against each other and they will remain at hard angles until it was all solved and the mastermind is dead.

Two weeks into their stay at the chateau, Jamila rose on her backside and watched her lover sleeping. It has been a long fourteen days resting and nurturing each other essence, holding each other for hours sorting through personal thoughts, and being silent. Most of the time respecting the other space as they came to crib with their life since they met and being comfortable with the silence between them. Liam worked out in the gym in the five bedrooms and bathrooms, a living, dining, tea rooms, and a cocktail lounge with a massive kitchen. Jamila cooked breakfast and read her magazines or from the books in the vast den. They had massages and lazed in the heated pool spending time together, however, also with themselves. They had agreed not to make love in the emotional uproar they were going through because arousal mixed with pain and anger isn't a fruitful productive combination. It led to pain and pleasure which led to meaningless sex, a good fuck.

Jamila had recuperated from the events in France. They hadn't made love in weeks, the last time was in the jet. She leaned over and removed the sheet from over him. She touched him on his manhood slowly watching, as he stood straight. She knew from the music he made that he was watching her. Liam pulled his body into a sitting position, whispering her name; he buried his fingers in her hair. His hands followed the motions of her head as she made love to him with her mouth from head to toe. He was riding the wind of passion. He leaned over and pulled her to the side of him. He gently kissed her shoulders, her back as his manhood sort for her exoticness. They found each other as if they were magnets.

Jamila felt the edge of the entrance a split second before she felt him entered her. She let him have his fun lying behind her on their side. He was holding her hips into place and he passionately moving this magic back and forth. She counted to ten and suddenly pulled out and pushed him onto his back. He came unglued at the sight of her taking control. He felt a spasm of sensations in this turn of events and tightened his muscles in his stomach sending waves of warm awareness to her heart. Eyes gazed entwined and bordered on pure wicked sinfulness. A smile touched her lips and the sexual energy perplexed them profusely as he heeded her climb aboard this magical Wang.

Liam's eyes climbed to her breast and he sat up and maneuvered his tongue on them the same minute she slid down his pole. She moved under his touch as a petted animal and in minutes the sexual energy swayed them to look at each other again. To hold the forth a little bit longer he removed his tongue and let his torso fall onto the bed making eye contact with Jamila. Her eyes sparkled with the remnant of passion and song that had laid dormant in her heart stirred yet again. Jamila moved quickly and taking his magic into her hands pushed down on it with her pelvic talking all of him inside her. A sweet-scented breeze blew in from the window touching her skin into a hot and cold sensation, making the arousal exotic. It was mind-blowing how she moved to his grove, how his hands anchored her hips ground against his thighs. Their mouth melded as one as they climaxed together.

The minute their heartbeats settled they heard a banging on the window and Liam refused to acknowledge it. He pulled his lover to him, cuddling as they listened to the continuing banging now on the front door. Liam recognized Simon's voice yelling.

"Let me in you two fucking lovers. Blimpy hell what's takin you so long? Haven't you ever heard of a quickie?"

Liam jumped out of bed, looking for his clothes, finding none; he took the cover sheet off the floor and covered his body. Jamila laughingly left the bed and headed to the closet and showered; she dressed quickly as she looked for a very feminine dress to wear. This is the first meeting with the MI6 and understanding what Liam told her about him, he loved a female feminine and he loved the ladies. She made the stairs slowly and saw Liam with a much older man standing by the fireplace with drinks in their hands. Upon entering the room, they looked up and Liam left his post to greet Jamila sheet still around him in a toga dress. He gave her a light kiss on her lips, guiding her with his hands sitting on her lower back to introduce her to Simon.

"It's my pleasure, mi lady." Simon kissed her hand she extended for him to shake. "Aye Lei, she's a beauty, a fine specimen." His other hand patted the one he was still holding. "If you two will excuse me, I would like to go and wash up for breakfast. Lei, I am starved and make it good."

"Let me show you the way, Simon," Liam said.

"Oh you don't have to fucking show me anything Lei, I know my way around here. I bet you aren't staying in the master room, are you?

"Yes, we are."

"I don't want to know which room you are in. I just want to know. I am going to take the second master room in the back, way down the road from you. I don't want to know what the fuck goes on in your room though I can very well guess." Simon gave them a wink and disappeared from the room before anyone can say anything.

"He's quite a character, isn't he?" Jamila asked him an eyebrow raise looking at the stairs.

"Oh, you don't know half of it!" Liam circled his eyes around with flare. "I'm going to order breakfast, lunch, and dinner. Can you please go to the cellar and pulled two mmm three bottles of red wine, thanks, love?" He pulled his mobile out from his pocket and made the call. A grin hitched one corner of his mouth and a dimple flashed as he climbed the stair to have his shower.

Jamila walked down the stairs to the cellar. She liked the set up that Adrian had for them. A housekeeper came in and tidied the place three times a week, food can be delivered from a restaurant and all they have to do is fixed breakfast and enjoy themselves. This is exactly what they have been doing, silently and quietly healing, sometimes talking about themselves and sharing the silly things that happened to them growing up and making passionate love again, with Simon here maybe not; they'll have to put that on hold.

They did the same thing on board the yacht. She knew the yacht was going rather slow and figured that Liam ordered the Captain to take his time. Damascus had a very good partner who owned a yacht of the same model and made by the same company. She used to go sailing with them often to the other islands. She loved how Liam found time to spend quality time with her even when danger loomed. She hadn't given any time to the incidents that led her here in hiding. Sometimes, it surfaced in nightmares, and Liam would hold and comfort her all night. He was extremely gentle, considerate, and rarely put himself first. She has never been in love with anyone of this level of magnitude. Their love for each over is above personal needs even in the mystery that lured over their life.

She chose the bottles of wine and added a white as an afterthought. The cellar was full of the most expensive wine and they have been enjoying it since they arrived here. On entering the living room, Liam was adding another log to the fire when the doorbell rang. All of them looked at each other and out came Simon's gun nodding at Liam who looked at Jamila and motioned her to hide behind the sofa. The bell rang again. Liam walked to the door, looked at the security camera, and with relief yelled, "It's Damascus."

Simon heard the relief in Liam's voice and turned and looked at Jamila, saw no sign of fear, he put his gun back into hiding; Jamila rose from behind the sofa as Liam opened the door. She ran past Simon and jumped in front of him into the arms of Damascus. Liam pulled his luggage from the outside and stood it on the path that led to the stairs onto the bedroom. She took them all by surprise as Simon and Liam stood back and watched the exchange between old friends. Damascus held her for a long few minutes, rubbing her back. Liam closed the door and moved to the fire, giving them privacy. Jamila filled with warmth, love, and comfort from her friend pushed him away gently, looking at him she said, 'Oh, Paxz it's so good to see you. We have much, much to tell you." She declared checks flamed in the pick. She held his arm pulling him to the living room.

"This is Simon, the best MI6 there ever were in the history of the British Empire." Simon beamed from the introduction as he shook Damascus's hand. The doorbell rang again and Liam went to investigate. Simon's hand on his gun behind his back; he removed it when Liam said, 'food." He let the two waiters in, who went straight into the dining room and set the breakfast/lunch out, and ordered dinner in the kitchen. The delivery men nodded to them all and left. No words were spoken, they are used to doing this for the owner and their guests. As usual, Liam provided the tip with a *"Merci beaucoup."*

Liam turned to the group looking at him, "Shall we, please," and led the way. "Start I will get the wine." Simon heard the word "wine" and his brow went up in approval and his lips craved a wide smile. After breakfast/lunch, they all help with cleaning up. Damascus put the dishes into the dishwasher while Jamila put the leftover into containers. Dinner was in the fridge with the leftovers. Simon took a corner watching the others as he sipped for his glass of red wine. Liam put the kettle on for tea as Jamila put the dessert onto a tray. The three worked in silence preoccupied with the tasks.

Quite a couple they made, both working without talking, knowing exactly what to do next, a rare combination, Simon looked at Damascus, who took the tray from Jamila and followed Liam out of the kitchen with the tea. Simon drained his wine and left the glass in the sink, turned, and followed them into the living room. They were all settled with tea and tiramisu cake as lunch fell right into teatime. Simon went straight to why he's here.

"I guess it's safe to say that we can all trust each other, eh Lei?"

Liam nodded to him. "Oh, Good coz I got lots to tell. Only bits and pieces, it's a start from nothing." All eyes were on Simon as he took a sip of tea and a bit of cake. He's enjoying the attention and suspense he is getting from his audience. He inhaled and began with what he found out so far. "Lei someone is using your toys," he looked at Liam turned to Damascus and Jamila, and explained, "Yachts, jets, and business for smuggling. Your board is involved in every transaction because their signature is all over the damn place even yours too Lei."

"Oh no! Now hang on a minute, I am many things. I don't do anything illegal in my professional or personal life, Never." Liam said defensively and with an angry frown. His smile had faded, replaced by anger that left rage in its place. He raised his chin and embraced his anger; it was so much easier to relate than his pain. His smile was not pleasant.

"Ah, Lei." Simon paused for a minute while he sipped some more tea. "I know that and hopefully him and her," nodded towards, "Damascus and Jamila, believe you. Someone who knows you well is forging papers to look like your board and you. Interpol put two and two together when your signature and several of your board members were at different places from the dates on the documents. It's good that you're spontaneous coz whoever you told that you were going to New York and you never showed up because you switched or stopped over for some fun or other business in another country didn't know that, the dates were screwed up, including the board too."

"Oh, hell Simon who.......?" Liam wasn't given time to finish as Simon interrupted.

"Oh, bloody hell Lei, it's someone close to you that you trust, and he or she doesn't trust you."

"I figured that!" Liam barked at Simon in rage. Contempt for the person who is doing this to him and Jamila was more than a small amount of anger that was building inside him joined forces with confusion; frustration flared into panic and then subside into more fury.

"They are using art-painting to smuggle cocaine and heroin. The North and South Koreans are involved somehow and as usual the United States Air Force, I believe is involved somehow."

"No." Jamila and Damascus said at the same time in shock. Liam just looked at them and squeezed Jamila's hands. Ignoring the remarks, Simon continued, "Who is Mannatu, Lei?

"Mannatu?" Liam asked still in shock from what he is hearing. "Someone I grew up with and we used each other homes and things, why? His stomach did a summersault upon hearing his friend's name.

"I have a gut feeling he's involved somehow. Don't go to Japan. I think he's using here as his headquarters. He sent a prostitute to kill me." "What?" They all said at the same time in more shock.

"Yes, at the airport. We went to a hotel paid for by him. I fucked her and then drugged her. I left my notebook with the wrong information on it. I saw her tried to hide it and it fell on the floor. She poured something into my drink. I excused myself and took the drink into the bathroom and drained it down the sink and refilled it with my stuff. I gave her some sleeping pills I usually walk with; you know I have a hard time sleeping. I gave her the wrong notes because if she didn't take back something to the jackass he would have killed her." Simon finished and drained his tea.

Jamila rose to her feet and refreshed everyone's cup. "I don't think I …. I want a strong drink." Her imagination provided pictures of what Simon described making her relived being a witness to the murder, New York, Paris, and the images send her imagination into overdrive. For instant disbelief lifted across Liam's expression and was gone as quickly as she identified it. He sat unmoving trying to manage with the images of the nightmare that had driven into this fatigued brain and them out of the living into hiding.

"Aye, lassie I agree. Let's get this business away and we can drink." Simon told her. He doesn't trust himself to drink more and tell them about his investigation at the same time. "They found cocaine and rare art in walls of the engine room on Sincerity. X my engineer saw some white power coming out through the walls when we were in St. Lucia. It made him sick. He figured it will eventually sabotage the engine and I would know. He taught it was the Captain because he's new and Sincerity's crew been together too long for it to be them. He couldn't tell me because the Captain was always with me. Being sick was the only way out. Jun was poisoned by the Captain. He didn't cook the chicken 100 percent and Jun contracted food poisoning. Jamila and I saw the Captain killed a man with a knife, who I don't know. My butler Charles tried to poison us. He allowed Jamila to see him putting the poison in the coffee. Adrian mentioned that he is living with his maid, Mavis. They are safe and retired.

"In Paris, someone used a U.S. Army M16A2 - 800m killing range, semi-automatic through the window that shot Claudine in the back and the bullet hit her heart. They mistook Claudine for Jamila and she died. We went to the Ritz hotel and the French police had the room bugged. The flat and room were Mannatu." Liam voiced depressingly and disbelievingly. Mocking glint captured his hazel eyes and inflamed them with rage. White lines around his mouth turned to red; anger etched around his mouth and colored his eyes with darkness; his features were stone-cold even the hand that held Jamila's.

Simon had to ask, "How do you know what sniper rifles were, Lei? It could have been a KATE." He turned to Jamila and Damascus and explained, "USMC M40A1with a 1000y killing range. The bullets Lapua 308 boat tail, full metal jacket, and molybdenum or "moly" - coated rounds as it is called with Teflon. Or a UK British L96A1 which it wasn't, it becomes too hot after the first shot. I think there were two shots."

"You taught me, Simon, remember when you were recuperating here for two years after one of your escapades." Simon smiled and nodded his head. Liam was up and spaced the floor. I kept going over and over trying to remember whether I heard one or two shots. The sniper was static as a serpent waiting to bite its victim.

His finger in the trigger was collecting sweat; he didn't hesitate. He pulled the trigger slightly as if he were making love to his M16A2 that never let him down. This weapon was with him since he became a sniper. The MI6A2 cut the air as a sharp knife would slice butter; in less than a second, the bullet entered through the glass window and was shattered with the impact.

"Jamila was there a few seconds when Claudine was taking the dry cleaning from out the plastic bag; put a hanger in it and was about to hand it, Jamila. Claudine was moving forward and up again tending to the clothes; as she straightened up, the angles and trajectories of the MI6 were ready to go except a breeze from the south was enough to deviate the shot. The bullet impacted her left posterior scapula; one of the bullet fragments deviated to the heart severing the Aorta and the left Coronary Artery. The bullet left the body leaving a destroyed upper torso, causing her death in mere 3 minutes. She didn't notice anything. It was one shot."

"Oh, you were listening?" Simon laughingly and proudly chuckled. "I'm very proud of you."

Jamila and Damascus sat upright in shock. Liam remembering her moved closer and pulled her into his arms. "I am so so so sorry, my love. I am blinded by making money."

Damascus looked at Jamila leading her head on Liam's shoulder and him comforting her. He turned his attention to Simon, who seemed to buckle in pain. He yelled, 'Simon, are you alright?"Liam and Jamila both look up and see Simon lean forward bending over in pain. Liam rushed to his side follow by Damascus and Jamila.

"Don't worry Simon, Jamila's a doctor she will fix you up in no time."

"I'm not a doctor." Jamila intervened. She pushed away from the intrusive thought of being angry. She hadn't rested because of anger and anger distributed between them and the mess of not being free to live her life all because of the man she is in love with for these past weeks, no months.

"You fixed Jun, you've to fix him," Liam said pleading to her. Concern verged against his anger; his voice softer with warmth. They stood gazing into each other's eyes and her brow clouded with anger overshadowed with concern and she turned to give her attention to Simon. Liam's anger of seconds before seemed to sprint when he raised his eyes to hers. Damascus saw blood on Simon's shirt by his stomach the same time Liam and Jamila saw it. "I'll get the first aid kit," Liam informed them and disappeared.

Damascus picked Simon up in his arms and laid him to rest by the fire. He unbuttoned Simon's shirt and opened the blood-soaked bandage. They both gasped when they saw the open wound. "Ya goin' to have' to stitch hi' up, Meya." Damascus told her, "Dr. Meya," laughingly. Liam entered the room with a huge doctor bag. He opened it and laid the things out on a white towel. He gave Jamila's a pair of white gloves and tossed a pair to Damascus saying, "She needs all the help she can get especially if she ain't no doctor." He put his gloves on and to her. "What do you need, love?"

"We've to stop the bleeding," she told him. She removed the bloody bandage. "Paxz put pressure on it." She looked at the things Liam laid out and took some needle and thread. She took some spray and spray over the wound that was beginning to stop bleeding. She began to sew the two sides together. She wondered how he received it. She knew he tried to fix it himself. With the stitches in place, she cleaned the wound and dressed it. She mentioned to Liam to bandage it all around his stomach. "Let him rest for a while. He'll be awoken soon."

With the tea dishes packed away and the medical bags returned to their places, she turned to Liam. "Please love, don't ever assume anything about me again. I'm not a doctor and I never was one. I volunteered as a hospital aid in London while I was studying languages there. All of what I know is from my summer working there. The doctors taught me how to do many things in case of emergencies."

"I'm sorry. It wouldn't happen again. I'm happy that you can do this many things, my sexy lady." Liam said jokingly.

"I appreciate your gift of humor, however...." Liam interrupted her by saying, "I only make jokes for a distraction from the truth. Jamila, I'm truly scared and afraid for all of us. I feel lost and I don't like it when I'm not in control." She leaned over and kissed him lightly.

"That's alright. We can be scared and afraid together."

"How do you get him awake?" Damascus interrupted the lovers, more concern for Simon.

"Oh, Liam show Jaxz, will ya?" Jamila excitedly charmed in, upon which Liam left the room. "Liam told me about him and what you're about to see." As Jamila finished, Liam entered with a bottle of champagne. He opened the bottle and when the "pop" took place, Simon rose on one side saying, 'I want some, pour me, ouch, what the fuck." He looked down at the bandage around the waist and said, "Bloody hell, who undressed me when I took a nap? Fucking nurse, forgetting where he was and lie down again.

Liam gave Jamila the bottle on his way to tend to his MI6 friend.

"Simon, it's Liam, you are at the Chateau in Switzerland with Jamila and her friend, Damascus. Do you remember?

There was a long silence as Simon lay with his eyes closed. They thought he had fallen asleep again. "Who took my shirt off? I thought she was your friend? Is she into threesomes?" Simon opened one eye and peeked at Liam with a wicked grim. Liam helped him slowly to his feet and put him to lie on the sofa that he had shared with Jamila earlier. He stayed by his friend side and gently gave him a sip of champagne that

Jamila had poured out for everyone. Jamila sat in the chair Simon was sitting in, while Damascus returned to the same one he sat in earlier. They all sat quietly watching Liam sipping his champagne and occasionally helping Simon take little sips. Damascus was the first to finish his, followed by Jamila. Damascus was refilling their glasses when Simon told him in a husky whisper, "Make sure you leave me a glass, boy. Don't you think you should spill what you know? I am weak but wide-awake. Liam, I am sleeping right here tonight."

"Are you sure you want to go on, we can wait till tomorrow?" Jamila sort of made a statement and kind of asked him.

"Never put off what you can do today." What he wanted to say was "I might be dead tomorrow." He couldn't as he can see there is no humor when there are smuggling, murders, and someone trying to kill you. Liam nodded to Damascus.

"Well man, de Captain killed someone who tried to doubled crossed him. He spilled his guts to a whore who gave him a joined, and he smoked the whole thing. She too was high and she told the next man to come her way, your engineer. De dead man was settin' up a meetin' next to the yacht so he can swim ashore and no one would know to get the cocaine. De Captain was going to blame Liam for stealing the cocaine so his boss wouldn't suspect him. He had planned to deliver the art, too.

"De dead man checked out of the house and found it empt'. He called de Yankee and asked for more money and told him if he doesn't get it he would tell you, Liam. De captain came ashore to meet him, killed him, and swim ashore. He paid the whore's pimp a thousand dollars to bury the blood and dump de body in a well. The pimp didn't want to do it coz he kno' when de police find out its hell fa him. Sa he tell this other foreigner who want to make some money to do it.

"The foreigner, Falcon, a tourist from Brazil found

Meya's watch and wanted to return it. He doesn't know that you saw what you saw. He was being neighborly or so we thought. He was hiding from the law and had the same whore as the engineer and de dead man Morison. Morrison had asked him to help him with a drug deal and he was hiding in de bushes on the opposite' of Liam and Meya was. He didn't know that they were de until they moved and he went to check it out and found your watch. He was paid five hundred dollars. There's a warrant out for his arrest in Sweden presently but no one can find him. No one knows where he is once he left Bim and enta London. I was there working with Interpol and the police to see if dey can track him, no luck." Damascus finished. He used Bim an ancient name used instead of Barbados.

'Well not to worry, I'll figure the whole mess out for you, before I kick de bucket." Simon laughed trying to imitate Damascus accent with many failures.

"Go to sleep. Simon." Liam ordered.

"I plan on it. Goodnight." Simon closed his eyes and was fast asleep.

In the distance, the Alpine peaks lay covered with snow while the river cut through the Lausanne, the ancient town where the food was delivered from each day; not long ago the river toppled over with excessive water from a heavy downpour of rain. Vue Panoramique de Montreux Rivera is on the other side of the town, along Lake Geneva, an evening breeze ruffled the delicate foliage of the trees while by the lake sloping vineyards border the shores. The half dream and half reality region are enclosed with small wine-growing villages that are scattered around lively town. In the Lake Geneva Region, Canton Vaud is situated and extended from the Jura Mountains towards the Vaudoise Alps with crystal clear magnificent lakes blended naturally in the landscape. Vallé de Joux remained unspoiled with mountain peaks, glaciers, and the chalet villages.

This lovely autumn evening cast a spell over the inhabitants at the chateau inhaling the pungent smell of the earth as it changed into the forthcoming winter. Hanging over the air drifted the charcoal scent of barbeque chicken from the neighbor further up the road from chateau D'amour whose guests were having dinner delivered from the restaurant Le Berceau des Lausanne. A fire burned in the pit outside as they ate their meal of Fondue with Raclette, Risotto with mushrooms, Gemischter Salat, Magenbrot, Trout for Jamila, and Rippli for the males finished with Schwabenbrotli and drank Adrian's wine.

In the early hours of the morning, they had enjoyed the cool cascade drops of rain that had begun a sharp patter against the window and grew into the volume that crescendo, thumping on the verandah and swishing fast and flowing from the lake to the river down the road as if the earth was thirsty. A cleansing breeze whipped off Lake Geneva sending shivers up the spine of Jamila. The moonlight from the half crest white moon showed a cold silver of ice in the inky sky. The shadows of the moon glowed and blended with the firelight sending sparkles on their bodies. The four occupants were quiet and thoughtful processing the facts that were presented to them the day before and waiting silently, each with their torment of the events that led Liam to Barbados.

Simon was healed and when asked about his wound he told them the Japanese prostitute did it to him. He had stopped in London to have it stitched, however, his friend had died and had fixed it himself. He said she had a knife under her pillow and after sex, she reached for it. He saw her and backed off it cut him instead of stabbing him. He hit her and she passed out. The sleeping pills were double the dosage, therefore he was lucky it kicked in when it did. Simon told them that he had changed his beliefs; his new belief is Iconoclast, a man who destroys all religious images and attacks traditional beliefs. He is proud of it too.

Jamila asked Liam how Simon received money for his travels. Liam informed her that he has an unlimited credit card. Adrian usually has a bag of necessary money and information for him whenever they meet. The bags are the same and no one would ever suspect that they made a switch. He gave Adrian documents to keep for him and Adrian gave him cash and new cell phones. Simon had helped them set up secrets places to hide money after the kidnapping. Simon had helped with the kidnapping and knew where money was in case he was needed again. Jin, Adrian's cooperate lawyer would be here any day for him to sign the papers of selling his corporation and would provide cash.

Liam had sleep downstairs on a sleeping bag with his

friend until Simon can walk upstairs to his master room. The first morning Liam walked into the room that he and Jamila shared he saw Damascus in his spot, holding her. A sprang of jealousy hit him; he closed the door and let out a breath, remembering that "Jaxz" was gay. Jealous was not a feeling he ever experienced or used to either, however, for the first time he swallowed a large dose and found out he is allergic to it. He had to approve because he can't give his ladylove the comfort her friend can, therefore, he appreciated Damascus. What she had experienced and is going through is maximum stressful and she needed to be comfortable. She comforted him every time he needed it and he took all he can from her.

Jamila hadn't mentioned or whispered a breath or showed any emotions of what she is going through with this mystery to his life, their life, presently. He returned to their bed last night and all he could is held her. He wanted desperately to make love to her, nonetheless, it seemed farfetched to even try. There are many questions and few answers as the mystery is still at large, still to be solved.

The four friends spend the following days sharing jokes, some very silly and took long walks. Damascus shared experiences of his and Jamila's adventure growing up and travels. Simon joined them most days sharing his adventure as MI6, Liam adds his many journeys. These were moments of laughter that they all desperately needed to pull through what they have all experienced in the last few months. Liam and Jamila didn't have any conversation about their relationship except for nourishing each other essence as their future hung in midair with the unsolved mystery. There were some sad and tense moments between them. Beneath the avalanche were unaccustomed emotions as the shock was their main event as other emotions jumbled inside tying their tongues into knots. Liam's chest still ached from the emotions that exploded inside him upon them witnessing the murder. He felt raw exposed and unprepared and out of control with devoid emotions except for Jamila.

A faint rumble shot his pulse in triple digits as he mirthlessly snorted at the idea that she didn't love him which had not entered his thoughts. She never declared her love for him as he did for her. A chain of emotion ranged from anger to love and disbelief slid across his face. Tension vibrated in his body, a muscle in his jaw flexed and he watched the play of emotions skimmed through her face and guessed her dilemma of not voicing whether she loved him. He gave her a searching look and pulled a figurative cloak around his feelings. The feeling of despair can often mean the difference between loving or surviving and needing someone or both. Jamila had seen the emotions run across Liam's face many times as well as his wondering about her love for him.

A thousand emotions warmed within her since the day she met Liam and after each battle of surviving the murder, poisoned, and being shot she arrived with nothing. Jamila knew she has feelings for Liam; the question was how much was survival and how much was life partners? All Liam is capable of presently is holding her close as she leaned against him as needed for his security and strength. A few times, he felt her trembled, and other times she fell asleep. He knew in his heart he had to let it be and whether they find different lives after the mystery is solved he knew as long as she is happy and joyful with her life he will too. He's very grateful that he had found love and more in gratitude for knowing her.

Simon was the spark of the party with constant laughter of his MI6 experiences. He shared the recent events of being capture by the Afghani people. "I remembered that I had left money and identification about twenty years ago. I had forgotten all about it. I did the same thing again. I had hidden my money under the same rock before I entered the town and retrieved it after I left them. I put the new money under the rock without looking to see what was there when I retrieved it, I saw the other package and it wasn't until I was on the plane I remembered the old bag. The name in the passport's fake, of course." Little did Simon know that was actually his real name, the one he gave to him at birth.

"How did you know to find the same rock?" Jamila had to ask, looking puzzled.

"Oh, I spend a good amount of time in the area not long ago. I know the rock because I planted a tree, a kind of cactus next to it, and the only tree there. It's small and it isn't detectable. I knew the town too as well as where is east and west. I marked my path with north and south. Muslims used the east to pray and the west to break their fast, the sunset. I had forgotten all about those people. I warned them about a US attack and they loved me. I just couldn't remember them at that particular time. I do now. The minute this mess is clear, I am going to remove the money and give it to him." Simon gave them a big smile. In the middle of dinner, he told them he would be leaving in two days to solve the mystery. I'm going to London and Paris and back to London," Looking at Jamila and Liam, "you two can meet me there. And yes, Jamila I am healthy to leave."

"Agreed." Liam nodded refusing to question his friend, Simon.

In the middle of the night, Liam slipped into bed and molded Jamila's to his body. He let out a breath and lay there beaming into her softness. He rested his hot cheek against hers as his hand circled her waist. He was about to fall asleep when he felt her turn into him. Liam became alert, lifted his head, and their tongue mated for a few minutes as they twist and turn to adjust their body to melt into each other. Clothes removed, he rested his warm cheek against her stomach. Her arms enfolded his head as he caressed the back of her calves and thighs. He began kissing her stomach and felt his lips on her warm skin and his breath on her navel, outlining it with his tongue.

Jamila' responded with a new musical note that made a symphony to his ear. He squeezed her backside and he kissed her pelvis as she raised it to meet his desires. She caught his head between her hands, pushing him down lower, and raising her secret sanctuary to him.

He nuzzled her with his chin and nose rubbing in the motion that felt the loving from all of the heavens. She welcomed his tongue into her and realized that this no longer a secret to him. He's familiar with her as she is with him. They have drawn maps of each other's bodies not from memory alone, from exploration. How come it felt still a secret as being explored for the first time? Liam's breathe whistled in and out as Jamila matched hers to his every breath and grove. He now gave her astonishing pleasure from between his teeth as his hands moved between her legs and pushed her thighs apart until her stance was widened for him to slipped one tender finger moving steadily then slowly and smoothly in and out from within her feminine channel. Jamila matched the motion of his kisses on the tip of her hot spot to the strokes of his finger. They kept the pace for a few minutes and Liam quickened the rhythm, covering her backside with his free hand raising her to him, showing her a more intense rhythm, pulling her in the hot wild pleasure of sensuality as she begins to ride the waves of fulfillment. In the heat of her moment, Liam lifted his face and welcomed her sexual release.

Jamila's heart beating to Liam's excitement of her sexual release, she picked her body up and pushed him on his back. She lowered her mouth down to his sexual organ as Liam's hands held her head to him. He felt her mouth as her tongue freed fall on his manhood. He made a new musical note of his own, as he became a loss of all free will. He lost all awareness as a series of sensations jolted his sexual organ into a place that orbits only around him. He drew his eyes shut and moving quickly, Jamila made a soft funnel with her tongue and then took him inside her mouth. Liam's entire body gave a massive spin of ecstasy and he sexually released in her. She could pack much emotion into her tongue that there is no mistaking her love for him. She knew then and there it was love that kept her bound to him and not feared for her safety.

Jin, Adrian's businessman arrived in time for tea the next day. They were all sitting by the fire have cookies that Jamila baked and tea when the doorbell rang. Liam pushed himself upon his feet and answered it. He guided Jin who he knew for many years into the living room and introduced him to everyone. Simon, Liam, and Jamila watched as Jin took a little longer and held Damascus's hand. Jamila didn't know that the Chinese cooperate lawyer was gay. She gave Damascus a wicked smile which he ignored and gave her a serious face. She giggled in return. This would be an interesting few days.

"How long are you here for?" Simon asked

"Oh, only until Liam signed the papers, there's a lot we have to go through," Jin informed him and looked at Damascus.

"Well, I was hoping you would stay for a few more days. I am sure Adrian wouldn't mind." Liam chipped in understanding the handshake between him and Damascus.

"I guess I can. Adrian isn't that interested in buying you out, Liam. I never thought I would see him despondent." Jin mentioned to them.

"That's because there's no challenge anymore for him. He lost the glory of beating Liam." Simon concluded.

"Thank you." Jin looked at Jamila as she gave him his cup of tea. "I have news from him for you Liam. I guess everyone knows about the mystery?"

"Yes," Liam replied, trying to stay emotionless.

"Well, yours and Jamila's family are all well. Your mother and the Paxtons are in the South of France. Adrian has his men discreetly providing security for them." A sign of relived can be heard from both Damascus and

Jamila.

Jin looked for the first time at Damascus since he let go of his hand. "I am glad you told your father, Damascus. Adrian personally met with him and bought him up to date. It would've been difficult to have them in France otherwise. The ladies were all ready to go home. Allan told them that he won a free trip; they were thrilled about it. They can't figure out how he kept winning things as he never won anything in his life before." Jin had a gleaming smile in his eyes as he looked at Damascus.

"That's my dad," Damascus said nervously. Seeing and understanding Jaxs uneasiness Jamila charmed in candidly.

"Uncle Kai will keep them busy with adventures. He's good at making them do what he wants when he wants it. He often tells them that he has one life to live and now it is. Mum usually gives in because she remembered Dad. Aunt Millie will too. I'm relieved that they are safe. I was extremely worried." Liam was relieved to hear Jamila's admittance of some of her distress. He liked the fact that she's opening to express her feelings and her vulnerability.

"They are having a blast spending all the prizes Kai kept winning."

Jin concluded laughingly looking at Damascus who was looking at Jamila. Simon sat quietly watching them and before tension can escalate, he asked quickly.

"How are Claudine's boys?" Simon never met her.

"Adrian got your note, Text, and went to see her sons. Apparently, her husband walked out on her some time ago, they have neither mother nor father. Adrian found Claudine's sister, Helene who agreed to have them. The two sisters had known each other very well, however, Helene has a drug problem and Claudine had stopped seeing her. He had adoption papers were drawn up and all the funeral was paid for and he set up a trust fund for the boys, Alexandre, 14 and Pierre 16. He told Helene if she quit the drugs, he would give her whatever she wanted; it's working. She goes to rehab which Adrian is paying for and she's a model aunt." Jin exhaled a breath.

"Sometimes people just want to feel needed or worthy," Jamila mentioned to him. "I would like to see them sometime, Liam. They can visit us after this mess is clean up." She looked at Liam who nodded and smiled with her. Jamila was sitting opposite Simon who was sharing the sofa with Damascus. Jin was opposite Damascus while Liam was standing by the fireplace leaning against the frame in full view of everyone. The fire burned happily glowing lines of light upon the occupants of the chateau.

"Why is this happening currently, at this particular time? How long has the smuggling been going on?" Jamila asked no one in particular as an afterthought. Many different thoughts ushered through her brain, nonetheless, she asked the only logical questions.

"From what Adrian figured the smuggling began some ten years ago when Liam and Mannatu began partying. There are some missing pieces that Adrian can't figure out. He was hoping that Simon would be able to do it. Liam knew Mannatu all his life." Images somersaulted from Liam's thoughts of their experiences together. "They went to the same school and parties, why would he use you like this and for or what reason? His place of resident these last five years has been exclusively in Japan. He has 24 hours bodyguards and rarely leaves your flat, Liam. When last were you there in Tokyo?" Jin asked him.

"About two years ago and it was only overnight. I have a board member, James Aton that goes there and takes care of the shipping business, was on vacation."

"Well, there are still lots of questions without answers. And why now, Jamila, greed; Mannatu is a massive spender and gambler. The people who are working for him, Peter Lamburg are greedy. Peter and Mannatu are gambling partners for over twenty years. They stuffed the walls of the yacht with much cocaine and heroin that it bled into the machinery, clogging the parts of the engine.

That was why your yacht kept breaking down, Liam, all in the name of greed." Jim informed him.

Liam was spacing the floor shaking his head in disbelieve of what he is hearing. "How can I be such a blind fool? I was concerned with making money that I overlooked many things in life, trust. I trusted the son of bitch and he raped me. Who's tapping his room at the Ritz? Who is paying for it?"

"Interpol is on to him and you are paying for the room" Jin notified him "What the fuck?" Liam yelled out.

"Adrian found out that he tapped into your account through blackmailing a board member, Ava Nimto who he deliberately seduced through extortion. He drugged her with that "G" pill, the date rape drug and took a photograph of the erotica nature, and told her that he would kidnap and killed her daughter if she doesn't tap into your account. She was relieved when Adrian asked her. She spilled it all out to him in a minute." Jin informed the group of people who are shocked by hearing his boss's findings.

"I presumed that you found the money Adrian left for you in the safe and Simon has unblemished amount to continue. Adrian says you know where it all stashed and if you cannot remember I am to say, Avalona and you would know."

"I remembered only too well the agreement and the code. I made it. I am grateful we made the deal. I guess Simon we owe you more than we can wildly imagine for suggesting and helping us with it." He mused looking at Simon. He had also filled Adrian in on the discovery of Sincerity in Barbados.

"Ah, eye mi lad you're welcome," Simon answered candidly to Liam with a wide smile. "I was only too happy to help out you boys." He turned to Jin and asked in a matter-of-fact voice. "How are Clyde and Nyles?"

"They are fine. Clyde is in Australia with his family and Nyles is in his home in Brazil caring for the farm with his family. The investigators they have working on this mystery keep them abreast of what's going on plus Adrian usually called them weekly. They know of Mannatu and since Mannatu knows of his family, they are keeping their distance and have extra security." He conceded. Jin put his unfinished cup of tea on the table and turned to Damascus.

"Do you want to go for a walk?"

"Huh, oh, of course." Damascus's taken aback was speechless only for a few seconds; his checks went up in red as he rose and added his cup to the table next to Jin. They both headed to the door. Simon, Jamila, and Liam were smiling and the minute the door was close behind them laughter broke out.

Simon left the next day. Liam and Jamila saw neither Jin nor Damascus not even at mealtimes. Today, they had left before Liam and Jamila were up. Liam heard them leaving since he had barely slept since Jin added a few more pieces to the mystery. His thoughts were living the times he was with Mannatu and he never suspected him of using him and his businesses for smuggling. He had intended to kill Jamila that fatal day in Paris. Jealousy played a part no doubt. He never suspected that his friend was envious of him, why? It was a good thing that Jamila was asleep because his expression was clouded with disbelief followed by rage. He angled his head down in her direction to see if she was still asleep; contented that she is, full-fledged fury leaped into his eyes turning them black. Refusing to allow the little knots of terror to tap dance in his stomach and Mannatu to win, he fought to control his emotions before it overtook him and he was out of control. He had no intention of obliging his rage toward her again. Liam had his emotion pike down before Jamila woke up, however, she had felt the anger rising in him as her head rested on his chest; this was how she was awakened. She kept silent about his emotions with the respect that one day he would express them to her. It is difficult for him to manage his friend's deceitfulness and selling his business he had prided himself in building.

Lunch was delivered and Liam went looking for Jamila who usually sits and reads in the room overlooking Lake Geneva. He stood at the door joyfully embracing her beauty, despite that she hadn't told him that she loved him. As much as he wanted to hear the words coming from her lips, he was overexcited that she expressed them during their lovemaking. He observed her body, embracing how fortunate he was to finally find true love with the most remarkable lady in the world. Apart from the mess he is in, he couldn't have asked for anyone else to share this experience with, and for that, he is very grateful.

Jin and Damascus were up in a balloon. Jamila was looking through the astronomical binoculars at them. She was focused on the picture she saw on the other side of the instrument and what she is observing that she didn't hear Liam entering the room.

"Oh, shutes they are holding hands ahh kissing. I knew it. They had de eyes for each other. Oh, baby……" Jamila whispered to herself.

"Who's holding hands and kissing?" Liam wanted to know as a brow rose in question.

Upon hearing her lover's bold voice, Jamila realized she was no longer alone and he had heard her. She jumped and straightened up hitting her head upon the plant pot that hung above her. She had to move the binocular to an unjust angle to spot Jin and Damascus that her body was position directly under the plant pot. Liam realized that he caught his ladylove in an uncompromising position; he smiled as he was taken in her peachy red cheeks and Jamila rubbing her head. Her tank top rest where her slacks began, exposing the right amount of tanned skin. She looked delightfully tasty as a Carmel cone covered with chocolate ice cream which took Liam's thought to a higher level of exoticism. He felt his manhood straight and he became red in the cheeks. Jamila stood looking at him embarrassed that she was caught spying on her friend while Liam looking at her all turned on.

Liam covered the distance between them in three strides and pulled her into his arms. He covered her lips with his and gave her a sensational kiss taking her breath away. His tongue tasted a spot on her color bone and traveled to her chin and lips again tasting wine and heaven. She felt her nipples tightened and saw him tightened down on his emotions for a short time. He kissed her again pouring all his love into it. After a few moments, he pulled away from her and whispered to her, "We should build our house in a very deserted area where we can make love without anyone looking. I wanna rumba with you al" day lon'." He tried to say in a Caribbean twang and failed miserably. The thought startled him and send him into a cascade of emotional steam. His eyes coasted hers and darkened at the stormy emotions he saw. She closed her eyes and fought against the strange emotions that coursed through her.

Jamila busts out laughing. "And I wanna hav' your babies." She answered him. Liam in shock gently pushed her away from him. His face in a question of asking if she was pregnant; he couldn't bring the words out.

"Sweethear' we are pregnant, six weeks." She informed him. He had bought a pregnancy test kit when they had visited the quaint town some weeks ago and last night had used it to confirm what she had suspected after her menstruation cycle didn't appear on a normal day.

"Oh, darling that's wonderful. Let's keep it to ourselves at least until this mystery is solved, shall we?" Liam asked her. He was over the moon with excitement and Jamila heard it in his voice. Collective with instinctive thoughts flashed in her eyes and it was quickly replaced with warmth overflowing into love. She soared to the summit of the energy of love that exploded her emotions and he was the radar that zoomed into her feelings with understanding.

"I agree." She kissed him with love and warmth in her eyes.

"That would be in the, six weeks ago, where were we?" Liam looked at Jamila puzzled and wondering trying to remember when their child was conceived.

"In the plane, before we came here, my lov'," Jamila recalled him, giving him a long sensuous kiss.

"We can celebrate, Simon's gone, and Jin's too busy seducing Damascus." Liam began to nuzzle her neck.

"Or Paxz seducing him." Liam defended Jin. She knew her best friend well enough to make that assumption.

"I don't care my love I want to seduce you this minute." Liam laughingly informed her as he held her hand leading her to their room.

The pistol PPK Simon had in his hand was an old friend he dug out from his buried treasure in the backyard of his old ladylove home, Avalona. When he met his ladylove, he had retired all weapons, excessive money, and history of his days as an MI6 agent. He had no desire to remember any of it; besides he was badly damaged when Liam found him that now his assignments are mixed up and just about everything else in his life. Aged he can hide it, however, it can never hide from it.

He looked at the pistol and at Mannatu all tied up in the chair, looking as a scared boy. His face was stony as a gargoyle with long thick laches framing his dark eyes and the wide nose and lantern jaw, brad-shouldered with a light stoop to his muscular shoulders betrayed his African ancestry. The expensive tailored suit with an ascetically lean lurked a cruel body with a gruff voice now delicately looked at Simon with hate in his green eyes flashed and danced with amusement. A sardonic smile curled his lips as he grinned with the delight of a boy seeing presents for the first time.

"I am going to enjoy cutting you slowly, you can bleed to death." He told Mannatu with disgust.

"For loosing and owing you ten thousand dollars?"

Alarmed sang out from the voice of Mannatu in disbelief. Erecting a metal framework, the way a road extended through towns he came quickly to grips as Simon's eyes flashed with pleasure. "I have lost more than that to other people and they don't want to kill me." He said with alarm in his hazing voice.

Simon smiled with a hint of admiration in the curve of his thin lips. "You have zero imagination Mannatu. The losing was nothing compared to planning your capture." He replied with disgust and anger he had for him and what he has done to his friend Simon and all the lives he disrupted. As effective as the strike of a snake, Simon walked over to him and sliced his arm cutting through the material that made his expensive tailored suit was paid by money stolen from Liam. Quicker than the snake's second strike he cut through his slack on Mannatu's thigh leaving a deep cut wound there. As easily as drinking scotch, Simon cut into his cheeks with the blade of his dagger, enjoying the darkening storm in Mannatu's jet black eyes. Simon's euphoria evaporated when he japed his knife into the enemy's body. His desire for revenge destroyed Mannatu's emotions and he is a murder of hate. The same as a bolt of lightning, the images of lives tampered with was burned into Simon's retina more so two people he had come to love, Liam and Jamila. They deserved to live a normal healthy life and not in hiding from a gargoyle-like Mannatu.

The taste of Mannatu's hate went through him, turning his anger and rage. As is cut into Mannatu's body, his rage turned into something warm, something that felt too damn good for something so sinful. The pain and pleasure cut across Mannatu's face and Simon recognized the same in him. He felt the pain and pleasure of cutting into this man's pitiful soul. It took a hell of a lot of planning to get Mannatu here and it was worth it. It was the only way he knew how to can get some quick answers; get it from the source, himself. Simon had to call on his CIA counterpart Milo Stevens and a few old retired MI6 buddies to get Mannatu to fly, well, drugged his ass here. Money can get you anything and he was happy that Liam had an excessive amount of it.

On this way to London for the chateau, he had made the call to the CIA agent, who told him he was going to help him; that was the hardest part because those bloody Americans are hard to figure. He couldn't call in any favors because there was none; the next call was made to the other MI6 buddies to help. They owed him and besides, they are all retired looking for excitement. The CIA agent, Juan Santos if that was his name, as good as his word. He smuggled Mannatu in a private jet to the Faroe Island. He had him over his shoulder as he threw the drugged Mannatu to the floor of the private jet and his parting words were, "I hope you take care of him. He's a ton of trouble. He's about framed and blackmailed everyone who's who. I did this because I want you Britts to take care of it. This never happened, if he is found it is on your shoulders." With that said he leaped out of the jet and despaired from sight. There was no scent of him in the air. He was a ghost.

The three retired MI6s who were breathless due to age sat in the opposite seats, looked at each other, and at Mannatu who was obvious to live. He hauled him into a seat and make took the rope and hand cups off from him. They sat back and looked at him.

"Hugh, we've to come up with a story to the pilots and stewardess about him. Check to see if he has any papers with him." Simon ordered.

Hugh who was the youngest of the other two MI agents pulled his six feet ten inches two hundred and forty pounds to his full length. Although he was breathing heavily there was a calmness in his round face and narrowed blue eyes. Balding and thick set in the stomach with his lips turned down in a grotesque smile due to a fierce scar that sat to the left corner of his mouth giving him a wolfish smile. He used to be the most handsome of the four of him, however, booze and too much fun created the duplicate he represented today. He walked to Mannatu and checked his pockets. Upon touching something in his jacket pocket, he reached for it and pulled a passport with some money stuck in it. There was no wallet. He opened the passport, looked at the picture and the name, saying to the other MI6s, "James Pickett." Hugh looked at the MI6s and moved his head in the direction of Mannatu. "It's him. This is forged," showing the others, the passport. "You think it's the ghost."

Simon turned in all directions looking for a ghost and said, "who, what ghost? That's our half breed drinking buddy that we had forgotten to pick up on our escapade. We've to deliver him to his mistress. Mannatu sole his name and using it."

"We have to give him some alcohol," Victor said who was the quietest and the wisest of the three MI6s and who was also the smallest and well into his seventy with dark green eyes, pointed nose, and narrow shoulders standing five feet six inches. He wore a mustache and has a huge white scar that fans from his left ear down towards this neck and disappeared under his jacket. His lips curled into an artificial smile and spread wide to his prominent cheekbone.

"Good thinking," Simon whispered and went to the bar. He pulled some Irish whiskey, opened the bottle, and poured some into a glass. He returned and gave it to Victor, who took it, smell it, and raised his eyebrow. "Good stuff for a dead man?" He hoarsely whispered with glinted in his light blue walnut eyes, his lips curled into a lopsided smile due to a mild stroke. Gray at the temples with black hair covering the oak tanned craggy swarthy face and a massive bulldog chest he stood strong to his six-foot frame. His words weight a ton with a quiet steely edge and the dangerous pestle gave the voices a seriousness of "do not fuck with me."

"Consider this your memorial service." Simon charmed into Mannatu. He affixed him with piercing deep-set eyes and a wide grin broke his stony expression. A gale of laughter broke out amongst the men. All eyes to rest on the shaft of light shining through the jet's window falling upon Mannatu's expressionless face. Victor and Hugh poured the whiskey down Mannatu's mouth. Simon sprinkled some on his clothes and next onto his pants where his pelvis rested. They resumed their original place and admired their handy work. James decided to remain quiet and looked on at the display in front of him, overjoyed to be alive. Simon raised the bottle of whiskey to his lips only to have it removed from his hand by Hugh. "Now, you mother fucker, we came out of retirement just for you and this is the bloody thanks we get." "What the fuck are you talking about?" Simon asked raising an eyebrow. Hugh had returned with four glasses and gave them each one. James took one and didn't consume any alcohol because he just came from drunk.

"Oh, that, sorry," Simon said a little bit shamefully.

"Cheers," Victor said raising his glass to them.

"Cheers." Simon and Hugh both said at the same time.

Hugh filled the glass with more and they had another toast. "To the good old times. To all the women we screwed. To the loves, we lost, and consequently, it went until the crew came aboard. The crew saw the six men and empty whiskey bottles. The captain nodded hello to them and told the crew to prepare to leave. The captain took one look at the men and the one tied up and wondered why there were only four glasses and not five. He shocked his head and chose to ignore it. He wasn't paid to asked questions.

As soon as the jet was ten minutes into landing in the Faroe Island, they injected a drugged into Mannatu's neck and the three MI6 lifted him into the rented car awaited them. James continued his journey home to London. Simon drove them to a deserted area he knew well from days of visiting his grandparent's eon ago. The men pulled Mannatu from the car and dragged him to the rocks. They tied him up and waited for him to be awake. As they waited in silence, they ate ham sandwiches they bought from the restaurant, drinking it down with the three bottles of scotch they took from the jet. They are flying back first class on the regular airplane, no one would suspect that four men came and three left.

It took a while for Mannatu to be awakened and when he did he pretended to be asleep; he can think about why these men wanted him dead. He doesn't know them except Simon who he owed through gambling. Whatever drugs they plugged his body with his brain is fried and he lost the control to think and opened his eyes to see where he was, however, all he managed was a very week, "why?

Upon hearing Mannatu's voice, Simon rose to his feet and ran the dagger through him. "Why, Mannatu, why? How about ripping my friend Liam off? Trying to kill them and how about all the people you rape mentally and financially? "That's what this is all about, Liam?" He was shocked that he wouldn't be able to finish what he started twelve years ago.

"Yes, you son of a bitch, what else you think? What did Liam did to you that you have to be this revengeful? Tell me, you mother fucker, tell me. Your choice, you die slowly or quickly, tell me?" It scared Mannatu how Simon's emotions had surfaced; every emotion hung heavy with intensity creating drama and inflicting fear, fear he never knew can be witnessed by others. Simon's eyes were an emotional wasteland directed at him and he was frozen to his bone with fear. At the mention of Liam intensified jealousy and hate surfaced from childhood was felt with a pang of fear. Heat climbed to his collar and ran down his spine; he avoided Simon's guarded eyes and the fire of emotions he felt with the blade of his dagger slicing into his flesh. By the second slicing, he couldn't feel the years of hate surfaced blocking the pain.

Simon was talking to Mannatu who was tied to the

chair with his hands cupped at the back of him. "You son of a bastard bitch, take that and that and that. I would love watching you bleed to death." This was an emotionally charged conversation Mannatu knew he never expected that he would die due to Liam.

Hugh and Victor had witnessed Simon pointing the gun at Mannatu's legs and fired two shots. He then fired another into his pelvis. Mannatu's screamed and start crying. Simon walked over to him and pulled his hair back. He looked down into the cold black eyes and said, "Those were for Liam and Jamila and what you did to their lives."

Mannatu's eyes swell massively as he recognized that he was caught with his pants down. He had to give it to Liam for figuring it out. He thought it was the Triads and his double-crossing them.

"Why?" Simon wanted to know. "You are going to tell me and it better be the truth or I will sell you to the Triads."

Upon hearing the name of the Triads, Mannatu felt that he had a chance if he told him what he wanted to know. He knew they would keep him alive. He's going to talk. Mannatu found himself staring at the barrel of the loaded gun after he finished telling Simon why he did what he did to Liam. Simon slowly emptied the gun into the body of Mannatu.

"Here is the story from all the facts presented to me." The tired-looking retired MI6 agent informed Jamila and Liam. "Someone has a vendetta against you or your family. It seems they had this plan for years. I don't know what it is, maybe you can shed some light on it. It has to do with stolen diamonds, a diamond from Somalia." Simon concluded.

Liam knew exactly what he was talking about and decided it is time to tell the century-old story. He looked at Jamila who sensed his struggles with old and new emotions mixed together. Although his voice was rough with unguarded emotions his eyes were soft and loving. Every time he thought he made progress with his life he slammed into Tilly's ghost urging him to be morally correct. Sometimes, he felt as if he was battling a hurricane all by himself, or on the other hand, he felt the same as the village's fool for not coming forth with his suspicion. As he looked at his beloved, he hoped she doesn't become angry about keeping this information away from her. Fear entered him as though it were a hurricane itself. He opened his mouth to continued and snapped it shut. He shook his head to clear it and took a deep breath. "I had a feeling it had to do with my past when I heard Mannatu's name. I thought he still held a grudge against me for not taking him on the trips with the other boys. We did not want him to join us because he was too controlling, violent, and drinks too much. I wasn't sure about the diamond because honestly, I have forgotten about it.

"My great-great-great-grandmother, Tilly was working in the diamond fields in Sierra Leone, no one would mention which one. They were afraid it can be traced to her and there would be consequences. Little did they know that for ten years I paid the price? She found three diamonds, one small, one medium, and one large one; she took the large one, hid it in her navel, swallowed the smaller one, and turned over the medium one to the guard." He took a huge gulped of his drink and continued, "Granny Tilly asked for her reward after the guard took the diamond to the mine master. Apparently, he told his master that he found it and to keep granny Tilly quiet and the other workers, he repeatedly raped her in front of everyone." He finished his rum and coke drink and poured himself a double scotch.

They were all sitting on the sofa Simon, Jamila, and Liam in the living room with a roaring fire having coffee except for Liam. Simon had returned after disposing of Mannatu's body and had drinks with his friends when they returned to London. He had called and reported that it is safe and flew out two days later to informed Liam and Jamila of his discovery. Damascus and Jin had left for an unknown destination which wasn't surprised to any of them. Liam had signed all the documents selling his business within 24 hours after Lin arrived.

"Granny Tilly went home and didn't go back to work. A few days later, the guard and some other men came into the house and turned it upside down. A guard way above the rocks saw her put something in her. He couldn't leave his post, he had to wait until someone relieved him from his duty. It was late in the afternoon and by the time he reached his boss. He came to the house looking for granny Tilly hoping he can cash in on the diamonds and not giving it to his boss." Liam finished his double scotch in two gulps and poured another double. Jamila's and Simon's eyes followed him, watching and waiting for him to finish. They understand his pain as he related the story. Slavery was a bitch!"The whole family was at church and a neighbor saw him, the guard broke into the hut and sent a child to call my grandfather and his brothers. They beat the hell out of him, the guard until he confessed. His body was found floating in the river two days later.

"After Granny Tilly didn't show for work the other guards that raped her came and searched the house; they have beaten both of my gramps, granny Tilly, and their two sons; they told her to return to work or her family will die. My grandparents and their son needless to say packed whatever food they had and left for good; neither one of my family have ever returned to Sierra Leone." He added with a shrug. Liam looked at both of them and sipped his drink. Mixed emotions ran raw on his face as he pictured a thousand times the pain his granny Tilly and her family endured all because of greed. Anguish laced his face in knowing the hell his granny Tilly went through and wished she didn't have to suffer the way she did those decades ago. Liam grabbed the back of his chair as he stood up and walk to refill his glass; it obvious that anger filled him. The bitterness had turned to anger some years ago and jaded his life leaving causation and a defensive detachment in its wake to people especially females. He realized as he became aware of his feelings as he walked back and forth in front of the fire.

Liam knows that his anger was preferable to Granny Tilly's rape and the misery he assumed she went through; he began to wonder what devils she had unleashed in him when he was told about her history by his grandfather particularly after they were a force to leave and live in exile. He suddenly turned from a grieving teenager to a very angry man carrying it all his life until this moment. Angered by the vision from the bruises and burden of knowing what granny Tilly and her family lived through he understood for the first time the fear his family lived and the distant of love they kept hidden and never letting him see it. He sensed it and resented that he was sent away to boarding school while his other siblings stayed home. The anger flashed hot and quick and died as full understanding came full circle; his parents had to do that because they were protecting him. A lump of some type of emotion that he didn't recognize or understood rose in his throat and he pushed it aside. For the very first time, something instantly sheeted his hazel eyes making them appeared the color of dense fog. He understood why him and not his siblings; he was the eldest and inherited the burden of the family's history.

As Liam spoke, several muscles flexed in his jaw, his eyes were braided with pain and anger that Jamila and Simon willfully ignored. With a grin smile, he continued, "Granny Tilly told her older son, Oya about her rape and to take the two diamonds and passed it on to his son or daughter. She told him to sell it when it is safe and cannot be traced back to her family. She made him swear that he would tell no one except one child that would inherit the diamonds. She died minutes later, and gramps never knew about neither the rape nor diamonds. He thought that the beatings were just a way of controlling them because that's what they do to others in those days and it was their turn." Simon and Jamila heard a light trace of anger still in his voice. It was dying as he related his granny Tilly's life story.

"Eventually it was passed to my father who gave it to me after I graduated from university in London. My father had made enough money with being an engineer, he never wanted it. My mother, two sisters, and I were comfortable and happy with what we have and there was no need to sell the big diamond. The smaller one was sold some century ago to send my great-grandfather to school. I don't know how he sold it or to whom. My guess was to Mannatu's great-grandfather because they were buddies." Liam looked at both of them and finished his drink. He ran a hand through his dark curls tousling them over his forehead softening his features.

While he was still tossing his drink into his mouth,

Simon picked up the story and spoke to him and Jamila. 'The person who set you up wanted the diamonds and revenge. Actually, he's the owners' great-great-great-grand fathers' diamond and the story was pass down to the entire family to hunt your family down and retrieve the diamonds. I believed that Mannatu's great-grandfather deliberately became friends with yours."

"Greed would do that to you. Hate can only live for so long before it expires." Jamila added and her voice shook with feelings for witnessing her baby's father's pain. More questions kept rolling through her thoughts, however, she stored them for another time. Silence followed as each of them absorbing the information of Liam's ancestors. Emotions ran across the occupants of the chateau faces as they came to grips with how the past has affected the present time with many involvements of people. Simon had made a decision not to let him know what happened to Mannatu and hidden the truth from them because it was his choice to do what he did. He had planned a story with his counterpart MI6s of what happened to him. He ran the story over in his thoughts waiting for the correct moment to spill it.

Jamila admitted that she wanted this whole mess over and done with this that they can enjoy the growth of their baby. She's tired of living life looking over her shoulders and having bodyguards following them around wherever they go. Liam on the other hand, couldn't believe how the past had shaped his life and he too wanted the mess over and done with as soon as possible; he can start living his life with Jamila and their baby. In the silence that followed, they heard the pattering of drops against the roof and saw the soft sound splattering against the windows of the chateau. They caught the glow of the fire as it danced down the dingy pane joining up with other drops before pooling along the ridge of the rotting wood at the bottom of the window.

Late into the night, Jamila had seen the building of

clouds lying low over the mountain, swirling with gray. The clear call of a hoopoe had pierced the quiet morning when she had cracked open the windows in the kitchen as she made breakfast to welcome in some fresh air off Lake Geneva. She heard an owl tooted and the sound of a dog's barking that had responded to the call of the birds now joined together in making chaotic music. Staring into the early morning shadows she knew that the grey clouds had turned into black water that would soon pour from the sky. The rain-filled clouds came down to kiss them with angry drops of rain within an hour which now spitted fretfully against the chateau D'amour. It had matched Liam's mood of earlier.

Beyond the living-room windows, they heard the stroke of lightning headed towards the lake in a jagged flash of cleverness. The wind clipped into the trees as another bright flash of lightning ribbon into the Vaud sky. A bolt of lightning tore across the sky followed by a loud clap of thunder almost simultaneous in the flashes. They paused for a moment to acknowledge the large spots of rain that came to wet the windows and see whether it would come dizzyingly into the room.

Breaking the silence and pulling Liam and Jamila from thoughts Simon continued as if the rain never came. They turned their attention to him as he picked up from where Jamila left off. "Yesss, yesss." Simon said, "however, jealousy and hate would send you into a tailspin to kill. Revenge anger is a horrible thing to walk around with. Mannatu is seeking all of it, greed, jealousy and hate all wrapped into one in a half boy's half man's body with no constructive way to channel it. He's a rotten spoil boy who got everything done for him with a very short supply of love. He spends money without knowing how much he has and knows how to manipulate to get it, even sell his body to the highest bidder. Lonely rich women with no purpose to live."

"You cannot be serious? I went to private school with

Mannatu." Liam informed them both.

"Well, he knew about the diamonds on his sixteenth birthday and planned to take it from you, even killed you for it."

"Oh God, fuck, this is insane! After all these years, after what they did to granny Tilly, they what the fucking diamonds? No, fucking way." Liam expressed furiously.

"What the hell does that have to do with smuggling and murder in Barbados, Simon?" Jamila asked puzzling a frown on her brow.

"Good point, darling', good point," Simon said to her. He hauled his six foot five feet frame up and out the chair. He filled his glass with scotch and Liam's, slowly turned to Jamila, seeing hers almost filled with juice, returned to the chair. He relieved his legs of his weight, made himself comfortable, and continued with his story.

"Mannatu ranked up lots of debts from drugs, gambling, and partying all over the world. He has gotten himself in a rightful mess by owing the wrong people money with a promise that his father will pay. One day his father found out who he owed the money to and cut him out of his life. His mother tried to save him. He stole all of her jewelry and sold it. This well soon ran dry and he was off again." Simon took a sip off his glass and blew out a whistle. "Nothing like a good glass of scotch, eh Liam, thank you." He raised his glass to them both and took another sipped enjoying it caught up some images that floated out of the swallow. "Well, he owned the Triads of North Korea millions of dollars and they told him he has to work for them. They kinda made it difficult for him to say no. They wanted to smuggle some heroin into South Korea and wanted him to do it. He did and double-cross them and sold them to the KPA, the Korean Pharmaceutical Association. He lived it up for a while with them protecting him until he screwed up again. He was smuggling anything and everything for the KPA. No one suspected a filthy rich black man traveling and living life.

Some countries are used to him and women, heh Liam. You know the life, you lived it. You even gambled with the bastard sometimes." Simon said in a deep cockney accent, sipped his drink, and looked at Liam.

"Don't even go there, Simon. I know the life. I am very well familiar with my association with "the fucker" and I've lived and paid some of his debt off. I still lived the filthy rich life you so scorned, Simon."

"Ah, good, I skipped the association and the time spent parting with "the bastard. You can fill those times in with Jamila." Simon nodded at Jamila who sat still watching the exchange carefully. She took a sip of her water and looked at Liam.

Liam had his back turned from her as he glanced through the drapery window watching the rainfall. He had pulled back the fabric with a figure as he glanced absently out the window. Seeing nothing of interest he turned to Jamila and said, "There was a time when I partied hard and gambled in my early to late twenties. "The fucker" was just a partying buddy and he became a friend because of the long family association."

Simon figured he should continue before any tensions arise between the lovers. They can do that without him."He got mixed up with some hookers in Malaysia. Mannatu usually stayed at the Station Hotel and carried on this business from there. He traveled extensively and played with every major criminal in the works. The corky bastard thinks he is untouchable to have gotten away with so much for so long. Between the Triads and KPA, he transports drugs using Thai and Burmese prostitutes, the same prostitutes he slept with, no one really suspected him. These prostitutes are called "flesh mules" and why it worked is because when other dealers died from an overdose, none of the prostitutes they screwed ever turned up dead.

"The prostitutes usually traveled on the bridge connecting Malaysia to Singapore is the Johor–Singapore

Causeway and in Malaysia the Tambak Johor. You want a body to disappear that is the place, every agent and every criminal around the world has used that bridge. There are very few witnesses or if there is one no one will come forward for fear of their life. The smuggling of gasoline, heroin, cocaine, and everything else is done through that bridge." Simon concluded as he fell into a trance of those days working there.

"How do they smuggle liquids?" Jamila asked twice before Simon was surfaced from daydreaming of the old days to reality. It hit him right there that he wasn't in his Cardiff flat; he's in Vaud, Switzerland. He told this part of the mystery without realizing his thinking. It was after he finished that it dawned on him that he thought he was in Cardiff. He swallowed hard upon the discovery.

"Oh, dalin' they smuggled liquids by placing a tank inside another tank as a double container. They used lots of copper as an x-ray inhibitor as well as it kept the humidity high for the outside container. It minimized the humidity inside too. Piece of cake." Simon concluded for her happy he is back to reality.

"How long has this been going on?" Jamila had to ask Simon.

"Who knows, forever, everyone is paid handsomely. It's a poor country everybody needs money to survive; everybody has a price, even you Jamila if you were poor and illiterate."

"I see. I understand." Jamila said nodding her head in agreement with Simon's statement.

"Come. come, let's have breakfast." said the MI6 agent.

"I'm not hungry." Jamila and Liam replied at the same time. They looked at each other and smile.

Simon didn't miss the smile between them, "You two got the fucking nerve to show up at my door at five fucking a. m in the morning and you aren't hungry? What the fuck did you too eat, each other?"

Liam didn't dare glance at Jamila. He figured for some

unknown reason Simon is tired because he is confused as to where he is present. He's angry about something that has nothing to do with Jamila and him. Jamila jumped up when the doorbell rang. Liam went and opened the door and picked up the package that was left outside the door. Simon's and Jamila's eyes followed him. Simon with a wicked taunt to his lips and Jamila with love followed Liam into the room with the package. Simon opened it and took a brief look at the papers and let them fall back into the envelope. He announced with surprising relief, "The official notice that my company and various business is sold."

Simon had lost his ladylove to old age a few years ago. He had met her some forty years ago in Jamaica while taking a break from spying. They fell in love, however, it was only after he retired that they lived together. Many times in the past, Liam would invite him and his lady love flying to Jamaica or he would let him use one of his homes for as long as they wished. It must be lonely as hell for Simon. There are no children who would inherit his legacy when he dies.

Jamila had pulled every container out onto the coffee table in the living room and was taking out positions on plates of Indian food that Simon had bought for her from London when he flew in last night at midnight on a private jet of Nyles. She turned to Simon and gave him a plate."I figured Indian food for breakfast and drinks are in order since Liam and I are such bloody awful people for waking you up at three o'clock in the mornin' considering what time you flew in. We apologized for our horrible manners and very grateful for all you have don' for us." Jamila said with a tainted Bajan accent.

"God, damn it, man. I sincerely apologize for any inconvenience we have caused you. I am taking you for granted and that is fucking bloody terrible and horrible of me." Liam added with a deep sarcasm with an African accent.

"I am an old man who has been put into the pastur' to die. I am dying and it seems terrible forgotten."

"Who would inherit your estate when you die, Simon?" Liam said seriously. "Do you have a will, Simon?" he concluded.

"No, I don't have no fucking will and everything goes to the fucking bloody government."

"Let my lawyers make a will for you and give your things to charity. Pay someone a light bill or college bill with your money. I'll see to it that it is done." Liam told him.

"Besides you can be our child's godfather," Jamila said and added a forkful of Biryani into her mouth, remembering that it was a secret between her and Liam, who started a series of coughing not because he choked on his food he was shocked that Jamila let their secret out. He wanted to wait until the mess is all clear up. Jamila paying no attention to him looked at Simon and continued. "Liam, we are NOT pregnant, you need to find some more creative ways of getting me pregnant. I am tired of doing the work." She winked at Simon who catching the teasing replied to her with his fork in hand swinging right to left.

"Shouldn't you be asking his royal highness his permission?"

Jamila is the one to start coughing as she choked on her drink because of Simon thinking. "No, I do no such thing, we're truly grateful for all you did for us and presently we can have some normalcy to start a family, well as soon as your royal highness gets it straight enough and start performing."

"Okay, you two enough. No, Simon, I agree with Jamila. You will be our child's godfather. I wouldn't be asked for anyone more plus we're

having a ceremony to celebrate our coupleness, you know being together."

"Coupleness?" Simon asked with a raised eyebrow at both of them.

"Jamila likes to make up words, she doesn't want to get married, therefore we are having a massive party to let everyone know of our coupleness, being a couple."

"I guess I am invited, huh?"

"Of course, and while you are at it you can walk Jamila down the.....mmm well bring her out from hiding and deliver her to me," Liam informed him.

"What the fuck, Liam, deliver me to you. You have to be fucking joking? I am not a thing to be delivered." "Oh! Sorry love, you know what I mean, I IIImmmean Simon can be the guy to walk with you as a Dad if you hhad a DDad." Oh lord, there goes I put my foot in it, Liam is thinking.

Simon says, "I am happy to do whatever you two wish, and Liam you should not talk. Be quiet."

Everyone was for the next few minutes. They finished breakfast. Liam went to the kitchen and made coffee while Jamila put all empty containers into the bag it came in and lay it to rest on the floor to be thrown into the trash. They had eaten from the plastic containers provided by the restaurant that Jamila had requested yesterday at breakfast when she ordered dinner and supper. Simon closed his eyes and was in a different world completely from the present one.

Jamila watched him as he breathes in and out. Liam entered the living room with a kettle of coffee, cream, sugar, teacups, and a spoon. He rested it on the table that Jamila had just cleared. Jamila pulled herself from the chair and without much notice to Liam pulled his sweater, planting a deep meaningful kiss on his lips. She tasted chantey on them and was licking hers when Simon interrupted them as he smells the coffee. He had seen the loving exchange as Jamila assured him that there were no hurt feelings with her in connection with the connection, "You think I can have some coffee, that's if you two love birds are all don' kissin' I'll also tell you the other half of it."

"You mean there's more?" Jamila questioned surprisingly.

"Darlin' there is always more," Simon informed her.

"Oh, then pleas' tell." Jamila pleased.

Simon waited until everyone was settled with Liam and Jamila sitting opposite and all were focused on him. He loved being in control and having the attention, therefore he's milking for all he can these days because this doesn't occur often. Looking through the slightly open window, the rain has ceased, and a slight breeze drifted through the windows sending the fire in a different direction. Liam left his food and added a log to the fire. He watched it sparked a few times before it came alit and shone a huge glow in the room. He returned and nipple on cheese as Simon drained the last drop of scotch from his glass before pouring a cup of coffee.

"There is corruption everywhere and this one is very old trade as the Central Intelligence Agency, the CIA, MI5, MI6, Secret Intelligence Service or the SIS or MI6, the Government Communications Headquarters or GCHQ and the Defense Intelligence Staff or DIS all knew of this, however, a blind eye is turned and I don't care a fuck." Simon took a sip of his coffee that Jamila had given him with some cheese. The spice was slowly getting to him and he wiped his eyes, forehead, and nose with the napkin before he continued, "wait till you hear this." He watched for his audiences' expression and upon seeing the raised brows he smiled.

"In Afghanistan at the Bagram Air Force Base is the beginning of the smuggling; it goes to Kandahar Air Base, and they moved the stuff, the drugs through Incirlik Air Base in Turkey, Aviano Air Base in Italy, Lajes Air Base in Portugal or Morón Air Base in Spain and it goes to Tyndall Air Force Base in Panama City, Fla. It's distributed to the bloody addicts." Simon raised his coffee cup to Jamila who lifted her body from the sofa and filled everyone's cup with coffee. She was about to sit when Simon informed her that he took four sugars and cream in his coffee. She hurriedly supplied him with his needs and quickly sat down. Liam will just have to drink his black because the milk needs refilling and she wasn't going to the kitchen; she can't wait to hear the conclusion of this mess. She loves black coffee and the baby will learn to love it too.

Simon leaned back in his chair and closed his eyes for a little while. The coffee in his cup spilled over and wet a bit of his trousers, which bought him back to the present moment. Without taking any notice of the spill, he continued with his story looking directly at Liam."Listen carefully, Lei coz this's where you come in. The KPA used Kunsan Air Base and Osan Air Base both operated by the United States Air Forces in South Korea. These flights go through guess where Liam, Japan, and over the pole, they can stop at Kulis Air National Guard Base in Alaska. Who would suspect any of this, certainly not any one of us; too long of a flight for smuggling in too many countries to keep track of it which worked perfectly for the smugglers." He had all eyes on Liam who had a puzzled look mixed with a question on his face. Jamila turned to look at him and realized that he's clueless about what Simon is hinting and she is totally at loss.

"You fool; you don't get it, huh?" Simon asked vexingly at Liam. "What the fuck? What do you have in Japan and who usually uses it?"

"I have a flat there and Mannatu usually stays there off and on. Oh fuck, he used my plane and yacht to transport the stuff, didn't he?" Liam more or less asked knowing the answer.

"Yes, you fool; he used your toys to do his smuggling. No one knew it was him; they thought that's how you made your money. It was well planned, however, the stupid boy has a little dick and a big mouth. He told a prostitute who told a rogue MI5 agent who told another prostitute who told me. Yes, I slept with her too. Long before I fell in love with Avalona."

Simon put his half-full cold coffee on the table next to

his chair. Looking at Liam he continued, "I wrote all this down in a diary I kept after every assignment. Yes, yes, I know I'm not supposed to but I did it so fucking sue me. "The rouge MI5 started the smuggling with heroin from Afghanistan and yes the Americans took all of the poppy and made heroin which they bought into America through the military. About three years into the smuggling an MI6 agent was loaned to the MI5 and guess who that was, that's right me. I asked for help from the CIA and those bloody fuckers didn't want to, ah they send a rooky agent, an observant who was already in Afghanistan some broke by a funny ass name Milo Stevens, of course, a fake name to help me."

"With what?" Jamila asked.

"I don't bloody remember. He and I figured out that the rogue MI5 agent, Peter Carter was double-crossing the British Empire, I killed the fucker and buried him in the jungle mmmmmmm dessert somewhere. Stevens didn't blink a bloody eye only laugh as if the CIA doesn't have rouge agents. Every country has some fucking agent that goes rogue."

"I trusted that son of bitch and he screwed me over." Liam spacing the floor and shaking his head in disbelieve.

"Oh, Lei he fucked you over, screw, no me lad, you been fucked." Simon informed him rudely."Interpol thought it was you until two years ago when Dominique Zenon told them that you were not." Simon turned to Jamila and said to her. "Forgive me for bringing up Lei's old love affairs. She gave them proof of you two being together when papers were signed by you in New York and you were in another country."

Jamila looked at Liam and saw his face was red with anger or was it red from embarrassment? She couldn't tell, however, Simon can. "Be grateful that she did. What did you do for her that she can do this for you?" Simon asked him because he wanted to know for Jamila's sake.

"There is no need to be so embarrassed and shock

at the same time. You should have kept your pecker in your pants, Lei but oh no, you've to go and release stress with an Interpol agent. She dumped you as soon as she got what she wanted huh? Was she a good fuck? Because sonny that was all she was good for, remember she is trained. Quit looking like that, will you? Be grateful that the fuck took place coz the last time you fuck her you're in Monaco gambling and not in Japan. That littl' pick of ass saved your ass. She told them you weren't involved and was oblivious of everything. Blind as a bat, I say." Simon concluded and awaited a reaction from them. Getting none, he continued with the last bit of information. Mannatu doesn't know all this as he only knew what they told him. He doesn't care either coz he gets what he wants and he's alive. The Triads have him this minute."

"How did Mannatu get away with it?" Jamila is dying to know. Liam looked at her surprisingly, what a good question and he never thought of it.

"He has a diplomatic passport. His father paid for it. The whole bloody family has one." The MI6 agent replied.

"Mannatu and some other bloody crocks went on a ramp and blackmail your board. They're all in it big and often they allowed cocaine to smuggle on your jet even when you were on it. They always convince you to have the board meeting in Japan every three months, right?"

"Oh, hell bells I knew they were into something illegal." Jamila jumped up and ran to Liam took him in her arms and give him a tight hug. She began to dance with him saying, "Oh, I feel so sexy with I am so correct with no evidence to prove it." She stopped dancing with Liam and returned to her seat.

"Yes," Liam replied, unable to stand any longer he sat next to Jamila. He took her hand and kissed it. "I didn't know any of it." He told her.

"I kno' and I believe you." She said comfortingly.

"I told Liam to sell his company to his friend as I had

a gut feeling that some' thin' funny was goin' on. They are all fired, as the new boss doesn't want them. Poor things can live in peace. I guess the Board is relieved and ashamed at the sam' tim'. Finish Simon." Jamila command him.

"Yes, my sweet, oh, good Lei, wise partner yo' got there!" Simon told him approvingly. "First Mannatu started with paintings that were a copy of the real thing. He started to soak the paintings with cocaine and use your yacht to smuggle them all over the world. He convinced you to use Peter Lamburg as your captain for Sincerity. He waited until your Captain was off on his honeymoon. Peter was greedy; he flooded the engine with excess cocaine which your engineer X found out, however, he thought it was you, he faked his sickness because he didn't want to be involved. There was a double wall in the engine room and Peter slipped the art in there. It was concealed that no one suspected. It went well for years until Lamburg got greedy and started to ship only cocaine and taking some for himself."

How can soak cocaine in painting and sell it?" Jamila asked looking puzzled.

"Darlin' you'll be amazed what those fucking bastards can do. Invisible cocaine is the same as heroin which can be done by using acetone, paint remover, and a whole bunch of other stuff to get it back into solid. They have doctors and chemists working for them, you know. These fuckers have highly qualified people working for them underground secretly. They pulled poor vulnerable people off the street to pay for their education in Biochemistry and Physical Chemistry with of course is a background in distillation. Pay them lots of money and take care of their family." Simon yawned and stretched.

Simon looked at Jamila as if she is the only one in the room. "No one knows these doctors and chemists. The equipment is all top class from the best manufactures. The place is beautifully done in remote areas, farms, and some cases right in the heart of the city. Besides, they have the United States Air Force Military Airlift Command known as MAC to move the cargo! Imagine that, look who is involved!"

"I don't believe it! All those rumors flying around about what America does is true. They created much of de mess in de world, why?" Jamila asked.

"They can look like heroes and save the world. Countries can turn to them and buy their products." Liam chipped into the duel conversation. Jamila and Simon looked at Liam as he continued, "It's all about money, money, and more money that speaks and bullshit walks."

"British and European products are of better quality than American, people will know," Jamila said.

"Americans well most don't know that, they love the inexpensive stuff, besides with America looking like heroes who would want to beat that. They'll get the market." Simon informed them. "Everything is a conspiracy to sell and make money. No one cared who suffers."

"Lamburg got careless and overloaded your yacht, Lei. The cocaine got busted and spilled onto the wires, into the engine, or some fucking way. I don't know-how, and I don't fucking care. I am tired, now leave, and let me go." Simon concluded. "What happened to Lamburg, the other witness with my watch, and the dead man?"

"Oh, that part of the smuggling? Mmmm I think I need more scotch, Lei." Simon grinned at Liam and push his empty glass out to be refilled. Liam quickly came to his rescue and as Simon took a huge sip from the full glass he sat down again next to Jamila.

"Lamburg had hired Morrison to help him set up transport. He got greedy and wanted more money. Lamburg being the greedy son of bitch killed him. His body was found in the well just like you said Jamila; you know all this." He looked at her for confirmation and receiving a nodded he continued, "Morrison who didn't trust Lamburg had the Brazilian Falcon hid in the bush and as the two of you love birds were a witness to the murder.INTERPOL found Falcon de Souza hiding in Belize and he confessed to it all. Your watch was given to the police in Barbados because they don't believe that you saw anything because you live there and it could have fallen off before or after the storm. Since they don't know about you witnessing the murder Lei, I kept my mouth shut and kept you out of it. You have to answer enough questions about your business and travel from the past 10 years to confuse the issue about murder."Simon took a few sipped off his glass of scotch thoughtfully. Liam and Jamila glanced at Liam silently, Simon continued. Liam shook his head in the quester blowing her a kiss instead kissed her ear.

It was a good half of an hour before Simon opened his eyes drained the remaining scotch to his lips swallowed slowly and added the glass to the others' coffee cup; Liam had emptied his liquor glass as they waited patiently for Simon to open his eyes; he continued looking at them as if the half an hour never lapsed.

"Falcon is going to change his name and address after INTERPOL is done with him. He told them that Lamburg would kill him because he knew too much. Apparently, Lamburg had a fishing boat from Guyana to stop and pick up the cocaine from Sincerity. He had planned it to break down and drugged all of you so the transporting from one boat to the next would go smoothly. What the idiot didn't figure was that Sincerity broke down before which I think X had something to do with; you might want to ask him. The next the bloody hurricane……"

"Iffier." Jamila stopped Simon and helped him as if he needed it.

"Fifer who? What the fuck? Who would be stupid as to name a hurricane Fifi?" Simon shook his head from right to left and back again. Upon finding out that it made him dizzy stop and remind silent with his eyes closed trying to stop the dizziness."Things didn't work out a plan. Sincerity broke down before the meeting point and Morrison was waiting there when Lamburg didn't show and the crew set sail for Barbados because of the bloody Fifi." A smile both hit the lips of Liam and Simon on his pronunciation of Fifer. Simon chose not to notice because he's tired, tipsy, and wanted to go for a nap he continued. "He picked up Falcon to help him collect from Lamburg because he has to pay the crew and Lamburg didn't want to pay him what he promised because he still has the cocaine and no money. Falcon was in a mess with the crew, blackmail was the best thing, the greedy bastards.

"Morrison's body is being cremated since no one knows where he lived or his family if he has one. Lamburg is in hiding somewhere and the minute he comes out of hiding INTERPOL will get him for murder. He still doesn't know about you two being a witness nor does he know about Falcon. Mannatu hired the sniper to kill Jamila for you can feel his anger and pain. He wanted to take away something precious from you like you took from him, the diamond. He also wanted to blackmail you for money and inflict fear that he can hurt your family whenever he can and want. The hired hit was totally professional and left no trace. He failed and he too is in hiding with four million pounds to keep him safe and hidden." Simon let out a huge long breath with a finale written on his face.

"I think I am going to go and contact INTERPOL with my lawyers. Jamila why don't you go and visit your mother in England for a while…. until I am free." Liam mentioned to her.

"I will rather be with you, Liam." She touched her stomach and looked at him.

"I do want you with me. My visit with INTERPOL will be long hours and much work………..tiring days. I think having your mother with you would do you two good."

"Ok. Let her come to Lyon and stay with us."

"That's sounds great." A thought ran straight out from

somewhere and Liam put it forward to her. "You are going to France where...."

Reading his language Jamila interrupted him with, "I am fine with it all. Time for us to sort out the rest and move on with our lives, my sweet lov'. Besides, I have you to lean on." She smiled at him with warm eyes full with love. "Liam, I am in love with you that I wanted us to be together for the rest of our lif'." Jamila leaned into him and kissed him. Liam hearing her declaration of love for him pulled her on his lap and kissed her until she had to push him away to breathe. Simon sat in his chair wide awake as he watched with love at the two people who mean the most to him in the whole wide world. Liam well aware that he was there turned to him.

"Simon, I have a surprise for you," Liam said.

"It's not the baby you two are having?' He watched the two surprised looks from Liam and Jamila. "I am old you two. I am not stupid yet. I am going and get change and you can take me to get it, the surprise. Just in case Liam thought the surprise will be tomorrow he said on his shaking legs "Now boy," Simon answered. Oh, how he loves surprises!

10

Adrian Bahar Al-Karachi leaned his head against the seat of his private jet. Oh hell, he is tired and felt older than his thirty-five years. He even shaved off the beard he kept the past twenty years to show his ego that he is young. It is not the business of Liam that made him old, that was a pleasure doing as he loved the challenge; it was his three wives. How the hell other men do it he doesn't know. He is overjoyed that he is presently divorced from all of them. If only he had listed to Liam, Nyles, Clyde, and Jun. He bought them three houses alongside each other and provided beyond what they deserve as long as they cared for his children. He has six for the three wives, one for wife number one Yurcci, three for wife number two Amalli, and two twins boys for wife number three Narria. He provided a housekeeper and nannies for each of them. He told them they could sleep with whoever they want as long as he or she doesn't live with his children and the children don't have any knowledge of their sexual affairs.

The children and their mothers have bodyguards for protection, and he visited his children whenever he wishes. He told them that he would disinherit them if they do anything else. Upon taking another husband, he would have full custody of his children and they will have a small allowance unless they have the new husband supporting them or they worked. They are all free to go when his children are all sixteen. Ah! The taste of whiskey to smooth the hell he has been through with those bloody women. He closed his eyes for a long minute and slowly opened them when the pilot announced that they have arrived at their destination, New York City, his last piece of business of Liam's to sell his homes around the world.

He glanced to see whether Jin acknowledged the pilot and saw him talking on the phone to his lover. He gave Adrian a nod and closed his mobile. Jin had been smiling since he returned from Switzerland. It seemed the relationship with Damascus is very serious. He was happy for them both, everyone deserved to be happy, even him. He felt a loneliness that slipped into his body and shot up his spine clouding his thoughts. Adrian bought his thought back to Liam, he purchases the whole business, selling it off in bits and pieces to the highest bidder. As Jin was having the legal documents of Liam's vast homes put together he was busy negotiating with others to liquidate the business he bought from Liam to other people.

All illegal activities will have to be stopped as the new owners let the people involved over to INTERPOL. He has pending sales for a few little businesses that Liam had under a different corporation. He had given the employees a wonderful retirement package and in the midst of that, he sold some of his business as well. He is getting too old and decided he wanted to have more fun and spend time with his children and maybe a lover to spend the rest of his life with as others have in life. Even Jun found a lady love Shana from Morocco where he had taken up residence after leaving Liam. He can see his life in the future and smile at what he envisioned.

Liam was watching Jamila's hands on her stomach. It has been two months since they returned from London with Simon who was launching at the pool. They had spent six weeks in Lyon while INTERPOL interview and collected evidence from Liam about his activities on certain days the smuggling took place, his businesses that were used for illegal activities, the poisoning, and shooting. Charles and Mavis made their statements on blackmail, kidnapping, and poisoning. Liam gave him a big hug and established him up in a nice villa in the south of Australia to live out the rest of his life with his lady love. Simon was with him throughout the inquest and they went to his place for the first time to sort his things out and move him in with them. They are renting a house in Marseille while their house is being built in a very secluded area with a beach view of the Mediterranean Sea.

Liam and Jamila had enough money to live on for the rest of their lives. Liam selling his business freed cash for him to be more liberated to live life, raise their children, and choose what they want to do. They have planned in building vacation homes and selling them. With Damascus living with Jin and traveling wherever business took them, he and Jamila had all the time in the world to get to know each other slowly. Their baby daughter is due in a few months and they decided to name her Tilly Adriana Nwosu. Life is great for them as they build their love nest.

"Do you think we can teach her sign language?" Liam asked Jamila.

"Of course, oops she is kicking. We'll teach her all the languages we know and our heritage too. Sign language?" Jamila asked remembering for the first time her sending him a sign language message. Liam understood the huge color in her cheeks, smiled, and said to her. "I am not a jerk for spying on you and I am not bloody rude." He finished pulling her closer to him as they walk to the house from the lake.

"Well, that put me in my place as you did when you think me a docta'. This would teach us not to assume anything about each other." She squeezed his hand that lay on her stomach. "I think I am going to have a nap before tea."

Three hours later, Jamila felt Liam's erection probing her back at the same time he reached for her breast and gently squeezed them. Her nipples rose to the occasion and he kissed the back of her neck as he turned her around and pushed his hips forward until he found her opening and entered her. Her wet warmth made his head spin as he moved in and out. He listened to her quickening breathing and matched his with hers. They developed a rhythm and he moved in and out of her faster for a while then slowed as she contracted her muscle over his manhood.

Jamila gripped the cushion on the sofa in their room and began to make loud sounds from within her. He was closed and he lost every common sense that told him to wait for her. He was out of control and let himself loose inside of her. Halfway through his release, Liam surfaced to hear her release too. He moved his hand from holding her thigh to the notch of her sexuality. She gulped for air and buried her face into the cushion. He felt her go limp as the last of him went into her. He lifted her off the sofa and held her as he lay down on his side pulling her on her side next to him. Not once did he fell out of her. She waited until they both were breathing normally. She could see feel the sensations from a double orgasm and her excitement grew. She tightened her muscles and gave several contracts on his soft manhood still lying quietly inside of her. She found a rhythm that sends an alert to the almost sleeping man next to her. He felt her contractions and was wide awake as he held her hips in place and as she contracted while Liam pushed and within minutes again, he was rocking her boat into a climax far beyond what they have ever experienced.

Simon was living life with Liam and Jamila as he was part of their family; He felt comfortable for the first time since his ladylove Avalona died, he felt loved. He watched Jamila and Liam planning their future with much love. They finally can live in peace with their daughter, his goddaughter; him a godfather and he intended to be the best one. He is glad he killed Mannatu. A few days ago, they were all sitting outside having a glass of wine when Jamila voiced what happened to Mannatu and if they had caught the killer in Barbados.

"What did you do to Mannatu? Did they catch the

killer?" Jamila asked.

"The CIA got hold of him before I did, and I don't know what those sons of a bitches did. I can't find out any more information. I think they've him in hiding and would try to have him tell them what he knows. I don't think Lamburg will live long enough to go to Barbados for trial." Simon concluded.

"You know it's very sad what Mannatu did. I never knew people to hold on to hate for centuries. My ancestors paid a huge price for slavery. Those bastards had much and yet they wanted what little we had." Liam said sadly.

"I don't think there'll be any more trouble from you, Lei." Simon informed the couple.

"Oh, Tilly is kicking. We're glad we kidnapped you Simon and bought you here. I don't know how we can ever thank you." Jamila smiling said to him

"Kidnap me?" Simon asked.

"Yes, I asked Liam that I wanted you to come and live with us and he said that would be difficult to get you out of your house. I said no, it would be easy." Jamila grinned at them both.

"What happened to my stuff?" Simon wanted to know.

"Oh, Adrian had them put in storage and gave your flat up. We'll have them shipped here once the house is finished building. You should sell your flat. Do you have any money in safekeeping?" Jamila gave him a wink.

"Oh?" Simon was grinning. "I would love to move in with you two love birds. I know you want a babysitter soon and I will gladly pay my rent that way. No, I don't have any money saved and yes, I'll sell the flat. Maybe Adrian can do that for me." The MI6 retired agent spoke in a deep cockney voice.

"Ah!" Jamila laughed as Tilly gave a few more kicks.

"Jamila, I need a favor from you. I would like you to help me write my memoir and have it published. It'll be a hellva one. The things I know about the British and American government is beyond your wildest imagination.

It was to be published after I died. Liam, I need a lawyer to make out my will." Simon finished.

"A will?" Liam asked. "Don't you have one?"

"I wouldn't have asked if I did. I want all of my belonging shipped to me as soon as possible because I have things that I need to take care of before Tilly is born."

"I'll have it all here within a week, including the lawyer. Simon, do you have any family that we should contact?" Liam asked him.

"No, no brothers, sisters, parents, or wife. You two are it. I'm very happy you kidnap me. I think I'll live a little longer."

"Oh, Simon, you are family, and don't you dare forget it," Jamila told me.

"Thank you, darlin'. How about my memoir?"

"I would be happy to do it for you when she isn't kicking."

"How are you doing, Jamila?" Liam asked her. "I know it has been horrible for you. When I look back at our meeting and all that took place, I feel nausea. I think of our love and our little one soon to be born, I want to say it was worth it. I have much more this moment than ever in my life. I am very sorry to have caused you any pain, my love." Liam leaned over, picked her hands up to his lips, and kissed them.

"Wait a minute how do you know that my Godchild is a girl?" Simon came to light with a question he never thought of before he figured they were pregnant.

"Oh, I went to the doctor with Mum in Lyon. Liam and I were picking out names for a girl or boy before we found out the baby's sex."

"Okay, I got it. Are you planning on having more children?

"Yes, a boy next time and you can consider me putting an order in, my wonderful lady love."

"With you buttering me with sweet jelly, my darling considered it done." Just for the heck of it, she added. "I think you better stay active and fit to produce the sperm for a male." She giggled and broke out into laughter. Simon joined her. As the laugher subsided a feeling flood Jamila and she ventured into it. "You know." Jamila looked at Simon and at Liam who still held her hands. "I was numb for a long time and didn't want to think about any of it. My nightmares were real as I kept seeing him killing you and me. Later, the poisoning and the shooting, I still don't understand why they wanted to kill me?" She looked at Simon.

"They were trying to scare Liam by killing you. The sniper confused you with her. I guess with both of you sorting the clothes he must have blink when the wind blew and didn't see the switch. It's the only logical explanation." Simon filled in the missing pieces to her question.

Taking a sip of wine Jamila continued, "I kinda settled down when we were in Switzerland and you." She looked at Simon. "And Jaxz, I began to release it all. I began to feel safe. I do my meditation, I've released all the anxiety and stress of it all." She finished.

"You know." Simon looked at her. "For the sake of Tilly, you've to be happy. I want a happy joyful goddaughter."

"Oh Simon, you'll have a happy joyful goddaughter and we'll have the same order to go with a twist." Jamila looked at Liam laughing. "I know that your love has pulled me through it all, Liam." Jamila leaned over and kissed him on the lips. "It helped tremendously.

"Oh, by the way, if the baby is a boy what would you've named him?" Simon asked with both replying at the same time.

"Simon."

It took Jamila and Simon years to organize all the undercover assignments and have them in a sequential order to write his memoir. Most of the time, Simon cannot remember one day or assignment from the other; they had to stop for a long period of time. They hired a typist to type the notes so Jamila can put all the facts together. All of Simon's different names were written down that he used for what assignments and of course he remembered who he had sex with, where, and whom. This was another long silence when he returned to his memory and relived those excitements. Jamila left the room and gave him privacy and let the typist take notes. She'll read it when it's printed in a book format. Simon took many notes, which left her puzzled as some were written in codes. It took her several weeks to get the key for the codes from Simon's memory, nonetheless eventually, they work faster as she read bits and pieces of the decoded notes. It jolted his memory and they move quicker some days more than others with his memoir. Later, Simon was bursting into their bedroom one March morning in 2011 shouting, "Look what happened to Japan. I can't believe it. It's a good thing that Adrian sold your flat 'cos it's all gone. Japan had an earthquake and a tsunami is unfolding."

Jamila stood over the grave of Simon. She looked at the coffin laying upon the site ready for burial. She had come to love the old man these past five years, no since he was introduced to her. Her hand rest on her swollen stomach, eight months pregnant with her and Liam's son. Simon was good as his word with being a godfather and babysitter. Tilly, presently four years loved her godfather, as he would take her to school, taught her to swim, write her name and so much more. Now, he's gone. He had lived a life beyond most people. She had started to write his memoir and had finished it a week ago. She knew what she had to do; she'll have it published and their son's name will be Simon Liam Kishore Nwosu.

After Tilly was born, Simon walked her down the aisle in a beautiful garden ceremony at their new home. Her mother, Amita with Alan and Mildred, Damascus and Jin, Adrian and all of Liam's family were here plus Xanthippos, Peirce, Orso, Onandi, Jacasta, Jun, Clyde, and Nyles with their family. The ceremony wasn't a wedding; more a union between two people. Jamila added Nwosu to her name. There was no religious affirmation only Damascus announcing that Liam and Jamila are personal partners after they exchanged words of love and declared what they mean to each other.

Simon gave a short sweet speech at the dinner where everyone was laughing. Adrian, the best man gave a touching sentimental speech. Amita gave a very emotional speech on behalf of her father Kishore bringing Jamila into tears. It was a beautiful day as it is currently. Tilly left her father and walked over to her mother. She put her hands into her mother's and spoke smilingly to her."It is alright Mamma, he lived well, and he wanted to go. I know he told me. He told he's tired and wanted to go to sleep forever. I asked him where and he pointed up." Tilly using her other hand pointed up. "I said heaven and he laughed. Mamma is Uncle Simon in heaven?" Tilly asked.

"Your Uncle Simon was always in heaven, my love and he goes to a bigger one." With that said they all left the burial ground, back to the house for drinks and toast to Simon. The burial ground was a plot of land not far from the house. There was no church service as Simon was a man who questioned everything, including God.

Simon Liam Kishore Nwosu was born and although Simon isn't here to see him; they can feel him smiling at them. They felt safe knowing that Simon is still with them spiritually. Liam is looking at this son sleeping while Jamila and Tilly are having tea in town. He smiled at the thought of his family and how joyful they are together. Liam walked to the window and peeked out at the clear sunny day. He narrowed his eyes against the sun as he glanced down at the building that housed the animals. When the sheep lamb in spring they would have four new babies and onefold. Bright yellow light streamed through the tree and lit the lake shimmering in the sun's glow. He glanced out the window at the lake wherein a few hours the sun would set and paint the lake in a glittering gold, a sight he never became tired of watching.

Liam moved the drapery a little to the right and more sunlight entered the room which glinted off his black hair while his shoulder was outlined against the glow of the endless lake. The sunlight drifted in the window and fell upon a crab. Liam looked at Calypso George sitting on their bedroom windowsill and smiled at the crab. He retrieved the memory when Damascus told Jamila that he bought a gift for her when he visited them in Switzerland during breakfast one day. He and Simon sat up straight as Damascus presented Jamila with a gift-wrapped box. She hurryingly opened it and left with her mouth opened wide upon seeing what was inside. She looked at Damascus and stocked her tongue at him with a scold on her face.

"What is it?" Simon had asked. As he waited patiently for her to show them what was in the box, Damascus was laughing heartedly with no regard to Jamila's feelings. It took her several minutes before she fully opened the box and showed them the crab.

"George Takei." Liam laughingly announced. Upon seeing the question on Jamila's face at the same time Simon questioned, "George Takei, the gay actor?" Simon joined in the laugher, Liam verbalized as if reading her thoughts, "I Google him and that's his name. I had to check out the competition, my love."

Damascus explained to Simon the story behind the crab. Simon ceased laughing and said to Jamila. "It worked coz Liam's middle name is George. Bloody Mary, who would've named his child George though Dick is worse." Simone finished.

"It is the Law of Attraction," Jamila informed them defensively. "Like you say, Simon, it worked. I met the most gorgeous man under usual circumstances, and I fell in love. How can I ever go wrong with that! Laugh all you want." Jamila rose to her feet and ran out of the room.

Liam looked at the two men for help. What now, when they both expressed to him together, "You better go after her and you've to show her love, lots of love."

"I do that every day. You think that would work?" He asked seriously and puzzlingly.

"Go make love to your lady and tell her you are overjoyed that she made the wish," Damascus told him as Simon shook his head, both started to laugh.

"Oh, got it!" Liam jumped on his feet. He doesn't need any excuse or permission to make love to Jamila.

As Jamila pushed the door to their bedroom shut, Liam was right behind her and caught it. She turned around at him and decided she was going to milk this for all it is worth. How dare he laugh at her wish! She didn't think it was so funny. It is one thing when Paxz laughed at her because she does the very thing to him. To have Simon and Liam both laughing at her with Paxz was more than she can stand. Jamila put on her best glare at him, daring him to move any further. Liam seeing her anger froze waiting for her next move. They stared at each other for a few minutes as Liam watched her slowly lose the glare. He was happy he could take orders from her because honestly, he didn't know what else to do. Jamila decided that she can't keep the glared any longer. It wasn't worth fighting over Calypso George. Liam seeing her emotional and facial expression changed called out to her.

"Jamila," Liam called her name as if it was a whispering breeze. All anger vanished and her love for him surfaced. Liam left his spot and approached her, she fell into his arms. "I am so sorry to make fun of you and George Takei. I promise I'll stop." He moved her hair behind her ear.

Jamila couldn't have contained herself any longer and burst out laughing. "It is kinda funny the way you say it." She confessed.

"Jamila, Jamila, Oh Jamila, my love." Liam bend his head and pulled her lips into his, pulling her closer to him. He bent to kiss the tan curve between her neck and shoulder and back to her lips. She gulped with delight as he nibbled on her earlobe, blowing gently into it. He returned to her lips, picked her up, and placed her on the bed. Jamila laughingly begins to tug at this t-shirt. He lifted it and threw it over his shoulders. He stretched out beside her and slipped his hand inside the front of her underwear. Jamila pulled his head down to hers and puckered him with a kiss of seduction as his fingers touched her sexuality. She made music that he is familiar with and made love to her, as his touch parted her exoticness, entered and discovered the core of her. She was extremely wet from his touch and he felt himself firmly rising to the occasion, beyond arousal if that is possible.

His slacks and underwear quickly joined his t-shirt. He looked into Jamila's eyes as he undressed her, and then resumed his original position as his fingers entered her warmth softcore again. He filled his hand with a breast as his lips sought the solid brown nipple. She arched her back plumping her breast against his lips and her hips against his fingers and thumb that found her internal and external hot spots. The fire of his love for her consumed him so much that being able to express it with his burning passion in his heart to her gave him immense pleasure. He kept that position, kissing her breast while stroking her internal core. His thumb laved her external core until she shattered as if she was a fine piece of china.

Jamila received such intensified sensations that the pleasure it gave her rocked her into double orgasm. Liam watched her lovingly as she tried to gain control over her breathing. He kissed the hollow of her neck, breasts, and back to her lips. His ladylove lay there helplessly and fulfilled. He gave her a few more minutes and then he swiftly brought her to him again into a sitting position. He sheltered her against his aroused warmth body as his hot mouth kissed her trembling lips. His hands sought her breasts then lifted her and pulled her down quickly onto his erection. Jamila let out a loud "ooooooh" as she contracted into him.

They were sitting straight, and legs folded behind each other's back. He kissed her gently, lifted her, still hard inside of her, and pulled her down as she contracted again into him. He is the one making the music as he completed her earlier symphony. Liam exploded into her throat as Jamila nipple his ear.   The lovemaking of the two-people merging in a perfect accord as one is true love meshing two hearts as one. The lovers reluctant to have this merging end know come soon again they would once more express their love for each other. For now, they lay together sated in a post-coital of pure bliss of euphoria. There was no need for words.

Baby Simon made a crying noise to see if there was anyone in the room bringing Liam back to reality. He put George Takei, mmmm Calypso George back to his resting place and turned to his son. They had donated huge sums of money to George Takei's project that fight for LGBTQplus to stop and prevent murders and focusing global attention and resources on ignorance. Liam whispered, "Coming, my son." He picked him up and laid him on the bed. He began to undress him to change his diaper. Jamila had lain out it for him. She always made his life much easier and more fun. "It is just you and me Simon, the girls have gone into town for tea." Liam completed the task of a diaper change and picked his son up.

Tilly was reading a story to her brother, Simon who was laying on his back on a blanket kicking his legs as if he understood everything his sister is saying to him. He was looking at her. Jamila was pouring tea from the teapot into her cup when Liam joined her with a drink in his hand. She smiled up at him and as his lips brushed hers, she felt something heavy in his pocket.

"What's that you are hiding from me, my lover?" She

asked him with a wicked smile on her red lips.

"I guess I can't have any secrets, even if it's one for my lover." Liam grinned at her.

"What lover? Are you cheating on me, Liam George Nwosu? I hope she's worth it." She charmed in as she sipped her tea.

"Papa, Papa." Tilly dropped her book and ran over to her father throwing herself into his arms. Hurricane, a German Sheppard, and Caribbean, a Doberman upon hearing Tilly's voice stopped what they are doing and looked up. Then on second thoughts, they dropped the sticks they were playing with and ran to Liam. Tilly was the first to receive his hugs and kisses. As the dogs arrive, she pushed her way past them and blew a kiss to her mother while her other hand took two cookies out from the container. She ran back to her brother laughingly and resumed her position with a book in hand. With her mouth full she looked at the picture and lovingly at her brother who's busy laughing and enjoying the freedom of being a seven-month baby.

Jamila smiled that her children and Liam were all engulfed in Hurricane and Caribbean. It was Simon's idea that they should have dogs for Tilly. They went to the animal shelter and Simon had chosen them, however, he permitted Jamila and Liam to name them. Jamila chose Hurricane because that was when she met Liam and Liam chose the Caribbean because that was where he met Jamila. Over the years, each time Tilly wanted an animal, Simon bought her two, a male, and a female of cats, rabbits, fishes, sheep, and horses. One is to keep the other company he told Tilly. They have a farm with children of the animals rooming all over the chateau. Liam moved his chair next to his life partner and together they watched the dogs wagging their tails next to their children. Simon was tired lying on his back turned over on his stomach trying to crawl.

Over the hills in the not that distant a rooster crowed,

a duck quacked, and a rabbit ran out to play with his siblings. Liam turned to Jamila and opened his hand to her. She looked at what lay there. A chain with a huge diamond, Tilly's, attached to it lay into the palm of his hand. She was astonished and speechless as Liam lifted and placed around her neck. "You can lay it to rest next to Calypso George. For now, it looks beautiful on you. It would be a family secret." He told her and kissed her lips.